D0449729

SUMMER OF SUSPENSE

SCIENCE SQUAD
ADVENTURE SERIES
#1

SUMMER OF SUSPENSE

Kristin Butcher

whitecap

First published on the Internet at www.cagis.ca in 2000 by CAGIS
Fiction © 2002 by Kristin Butcher
Non-fiction © 2002 by Kristin Butcher, Larissa Vingilis-Jaremko and Evelyn Vingilis, PhD
Whitecap Books
Second printing 2004

All rights reserved. No part of this publication may be reproduced, stored in a retrieval
system, or transmitted in any form or by any means, electronic, mechanical, photo-
copying, recording or otherwise, without prior written permission from the publisher.
For more information, contact Whitecap Books, 351 Lynn Avenue, North Vancouver,
BC, V7J 2C4.

Edited by Carolyn Bateman
Proofread by Elizabeth McLean
Cover design and interior illustrations by Jacqui Thomas
Cover photo by Robert Essel NYC / CORBIS Stock Market / MAGMA
Interior design by Margaret Lee / bamboosilk.com

Printed and bound in Canada by Webcom

National Library of Canada Cataloguing in Publication Data

Butcher, Kristin
    Summer of suspense

    (Science squad adventures ; 1)
    ISBN 1-55285-362-4

    I. Title. II. Series: Butcher, Kristin. Science squad adventures; 1.

PS8553.U6972S95 2002   jC813'.54   C2002-910923-X
PZ7.B9712Su 2002

The publisher acknowledges the support of the Canada Council and the Cultural
Services Branch of the Government of British Columbia in making this publication
possible. We acknowledge the financial support of the Government of Canada through
the Book Publishing Industry Development Program for our publishing activities.

Young scientists should check with an adult before starting any experiments
in this book

The inside pages of this book are 100% recycled, processed chlorine-free paper with
40% post-consumer content. For more information, visit Markets Initiative's website:
www.oldgrowthfree.com.

for Larissa

Contents

About the Canadian Association for Girls In Science

The Canadian Association for Girls In Science (CAGIS) is an association for girls by girls. The purpose of CAGIS is to promote, educate and support interest and confidence in science, technology, engineering and mathematics (STEM) among girls. CAGIS was started in 1992 by Larissa Vingilis-Jaremko at age nine, when she became concerned that many girls were becoming turned off science at an early age. Yet Vingilis-Jaremko realized that science literacy is critical for society's survival in the twenty-first century. She decided to start a science club to encourage girls' interest in STEM.

Where local CAGIS chapters exist, CAGIS members meet monthly during the school year. In a girls-only, social and supportive environment, CAGIS members explore STEM. Members have the opportunity to meet professional women who are working with STEM daily. Members are as likely to meet with a microbiologist and learn about the science of microbes as they are to meet with an artist and learn about the science of print-making. Plenty of time is spent doing hands-on activities. The ultimate goal is to help girls appreciate how STEM surrounds us and is used in everything, and how critical it is to our understanding of the world.

As part of the yearly membership, CAGIS members receive a quarterly newsletter, and a one-year subscription to *YES Mag*— Canada's science magazine for young people. CAGIS members also develop their writing and leadership skills by helping run CAGIS and by writing up their CAGIS events and other stories for the newsletters and the feature column in *YES Mag* called "What's Up at CAGIS?" CAGIS has an interactive website, where CAGIS members can connect with other members across Canada and the world. The website is especially important for members who do not live near a CAGIS chapter site. It has both a public site and a private site, which has a password secure "Clubhouse" for CAGIS members only so that they can safely and comfortably use the computer. The Clubhouse includes regularly changing features of Professor Hootie's Did You Know? column, great Canadians in science, Science Squad Webisodes, STEM games, STEM activities and experiments, and a message board where members can share ideas, jokes, stories, find science penpals, and more.

Since CAGIS's inception in 1992, CAGIS has had over 3000 members across Canada and internationally. Surveys conducted by CAGIS have found a positive impact on members' knowledge of STEM and on school science. To learn more about CAGIS check: **www.cagis.ca**

1

Fuzzy Pickles

The aquarium trip had been Gina's idea. It was such a gorgeous July day that Sue would rather have gone to the beach to try out her new sailboard, and Nicole would have preferred a trek through the corn maze at a nearby farm, but Gina had won out. So when the aquarium opened its doors at one o'clock, the three members of the Science Squad were waiting in line with what seemed like half the city. Once inside, Nicole and Sue quickly tired of watching the exotic fish as Gina read about their feeding habits, and went exploring on their own.

The girls weren't really a Science Squad, of course—well, not officially anyway. There was no secret handshake or membership card—unless you counted their CAGIS cards. Science Squad was just a nickname the kids at school had given them because of their interest in science. That and the uncanny knack they had for landing in trouble and then using science to get out of it again.

The aquarium was so crowded that Nicole and Sue had to dodge several clumps of people to get to the next exhibit. Right away a sleek grey dolphin swam toward the glass, and Sue aimed her camera at it.

"Smile," she said.

As if it understood, the dolphin's mouth parted into a wide grin.

Nicole groaned and rolled her eyes. "What a show-off."

"No, he's not," Sue defended the dolphin. "He's just friendly." She nodded toward the aquarium window. "Stand next to him, and I'll take your picture."

"Okay," Nicole said, beaming. She moved in close and crossed her eyes.

"Perfect," Sue said, snapping the shot.

"Hey!" Nicole protested as the flash went off. "I was just goofing around."

"Oh, really?" Sue teased. "You looked pretty normal to me."

"Very funny." Nicole made a face. "Take a proper picture." Then she ran her fingers through her springy black curls and struck a pose.

Unable to resist teasing her friend further, Sue peered over the top of her camera and jibed, "Are you sure you don't want to stick straws up your nose first?"

Nicole's eyes narrowed into a glare, and Sue took a step backward. "Just kidding," she said quickly. She raised her camera again and looked through the viewfinder. "On three, say fuzzy pickles. One, two, three…"

"Fuzzy pickles." Nicole grinned at the camera. Her good humour restored once more, she turned sideways and puckered up as if she was giving the dolphin a kiss.

"Good one," Sue said, catching that shot too.

Then the girls waved at the dolphin and wandered off to the next exhibit.

"What's with all the pictures anyway?" Nicole asked. "You must've used up two rolls of film in this place."

Sue held up some fingers. "Three actually."

Nicole shut her eyes and shook her head. "This can only mean one thing—you've changed hobbies again. Tai Chi is out and photography is in. Now you're going to be a photojournalist for *National Geographic*."

Sue shrugged. "Maybe I am. Maybe I'm not. But if I don't try different stuff, how will I know what I like?" Then she turned her camera on a crowd of people milling in front of one of the displays.

Her Science Squad friends were always teasing her about her many interests, so Sue wasn't bothered by Nicole's sarcasm. In fact, she found the other girl's suggestion intriguing—working for *National Geographic* would be a great way to combine her interest in photography with her love of biology. Just think of the experiences she would have! Safaris into the lost jungles of Africa, mountain treks into the Himalayas, white water rafting down—

A voice over the loudspeaker interrupted her daydream. "A man's gold watch has been lost in the aquarium. If anyone has found it, please bring it to the information booth in the main foyer."

"Yikes!" Nicole yelped, glancing at her own watch.

Sue lowered her camera. "What's the matter?"

"We're late! We were supposed to meet Gina at the shellfish exhibit ten minutes ago."

• • •

"Where have you two been?" Gina flipped her long black hair away from her face and then jammed her hands onto her hips as Sue and Nicole skidded to a stop. At fourteen, Gina was two years older than the other two and sometimes tended to get bossy. Her round brown eyes narrowed into an accusing glare. "I was just getting ready to have security page you. Not that it matters now. We've probably already missed our bus." Then without waiting for a reply, she bolted for the exit, calling over her shoulder, "Hurry up. We don't have time to—"

But her sentence was cut short as she slammed into a man crossing her path. Caught off balance, she reached out to break her fall, knocking the man's sunglasses off his face in the process.

"Oh, gosh! I'm sorry," Gina apologized, retrieving the glasses from the floor. "I wasn't looking where I was going."

"Don't worry about it," the man said, staring past her. And then he smiled. "Neither was I."

Gina held the glasses out to him, but the man made no move to take them.

"Your glasses?" she prompted him.

But instead of reaching for them, the man held out his open palm.

That's when Sue noticed the dog standing quietly by the man's side and the white cane in his hand. She tried to catch Gina's attention. *He's blind*, she mouthed.

• • •

"I have never been so embarrassed in my entire life," Gina groaned as the three left the man and hurried on their way.

"Why?" Sue asked. "Because you nearly decked the guy? Or because he was blind?"

Gina yanked on one of Sue's blonde pigtails. "Both, smarty."

A disturbance in the foyer forced the trio to stop again. A man and a woman—obviously agitated—were blocking the exit, jabbering and waving their arms at a security guard who was trying unsuccessfully to calm them down.

"Of course, I'm sure I had it when I came in!" the woman huffed. "And, no, I did not misplace it! I'm telling you—someone *stole* my purse! I put it down for two seconds, and when I went to pick it up again, it was gone. I had over $300 in that purse!"

"Don't just stand there!" the man shouted at the security guard. "Block off the exits! Conduct a search! Arrest someone!"

"I'm afraid I can't do that, sir," the security guard mumbled apologetically, shuffling the man and woman to the side.

"Well, you better do something! If *you* have no authority, call the police!" The man's face was so close to the security guard's that their noses were almost touching.

Sue raised her camera but barely had time to bring the argument into focus before Gina was dragging her out the door.

Sue was instantly blinded by sunlight. Shielding her eyes with one hand, she squinted toward the curb and then down the street. Their bus was crossing the intersection. They'd just missed it. If Gina hadn't mowed down that blind man, they probably would have been on time. But there was no way Sue was going to point that out. She was in enough hot water as it was.

Sue and Nicole exchanged guilty grimaces. Gina glowered at them for a second and then, with an exasperated sigh, pulled out the bus schedule.

"When's the next bus?" Nicole asked.

"Four-fifteen," Gina grumbled.

"That's not so bad!" Sue offered optimistically.

"How do you figure? We have to wait another half hour. It's going to be suppertime before we get home."

Sue shrugged. "What's so terrible about that? The sun is shining and there's a bench right over there for us to sit on. We'll have a nice, relaxing wait. The time will zip by before we know it," she beamed.

"I know what would really make the time fly," Nicole suggested,

SIGHT AND BLINDNESS

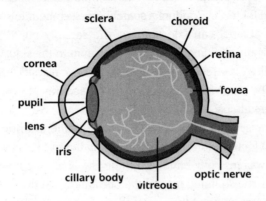

How do we see? Light travels into our eyes through the pupil, which is a small hole in the iris (the coloured part of the eye). The iris changes the size of the pupil according to the amount of light available. The light then travels through the lens (like the lens in a camera), which focuses the picture on the light-sensitive cells lining the back of the eye (the retina). These light-sensitive cells on the retina are called cones and rods. The cones are sensitive to colour while the rods are sensitive to light and dark. While we're out in the world during the day, our cones are doing most of the work to differentiate between colours. But at night in the dark, our rods are at work picking up subtle bits of light and dark. The information that the rods and cones pick up is transferred to the optic nerve, which carries the information to the brain for processing.

Blindness can happen many different ways. Some people are born with deformities to their eyes, while others may become blind as a result of an accident or illness. Sometimes people go blind as they age.

Two of the most common causes of blindness are cataracts and macular degeneration. When people develop cataracts, the lenses of their eyes become cloudy. This is easy to repair. A cut is made in the cornea, the cloudy lens is removed, and a new plastic lens is put into place. The new synthetic lens will never get cloudy. Nowadays laser surgery is often used to correct cataract problems.

Macular degeneration occurs when the central retina (macula) starts to deteriorate or work improperly. This is caused by loss or misplacement of blood vessels in the area of the retina. Though laser surgery can be used effectively for some cases of macular degeneration, the condition is generally not correctable—yet!

pointing down the block. "We could check out some of those stores."

"No way!" Gina said flatly, marching toward the wooden bench. "Knowing you two, you'll forget about the time again, and we'll miss the next bus too."

Sue thought Gina was being a bit harsh, but since she was already in the doghouse, she decided not to argue the point. Instead

AUDIBLE TRAFFIC SIGNALS

Could you walk to school or a friend's house with your eyes closed? Just *thinking* about attempting something so dangerous is enough to make a person break into a sweat.

And yet blind people do it all the time. Every day they ride buses, march down bustling city streets, and cross busy intersections.

When sighted children learn to cross a street, they are told to stop, look, and listen. It's the same for blind people—without the "look" part. Blind people must rely on their ears to tell them things the rest of us discover through our eyes.

This is where science comes in. To make street travel safer and easier for blind pedestrians, medical engineers have invented audible traffic signals.

Sighted pedestrians know to cross the road when the word "Walk" appears in the lower window of the traffic signal box. Blind people must wait for a sound instead—either a cuckoo or a chirp.

The cuckoo sound tells pedestrians it is safe to cross an intersection when travelling in the direction of the heaviest traffic flow. However, this is different in every city. In Winnipeg, for

she slid onto the bench with her friends and turned her attention to the people walking by. Considering that everyone she saw had two legs, it was amazing how differently they all moved—skipping, bouncing, shuffling, gliding, scurrying, clomping, limping. It seemed there were as many ways of walking as there were people.

instance, the main thoroughfares run east/west so the cuckoo indicates when it is safe to cross intersections in those directions. In Toronto, the traffic flow is heaviest in a north/south direction. So those are regulated by the cuckoo.

The sound for the less busy crossing direction is a chirp.

If a blind pedestrian is in any doubt about which direction is regulated by which sound, the surge of traffic is also a good clue. Once the cuckoo or chirp has begun, they know which direction the traffic will be moving and that it is safe to cross.

Even with audible traffic signals, walking "blind" may seem like a scary prospect, but sightless people develop their other senses to compensate for their loss of vision, and they learn much more from listening than sighted people do. They are attuned to sounds most people don't even notice.

How observant are you—without your eyes? With a friend, take turns blindfolding each other and doing some everyday activities like walking through your house, tying your shoes, or brushing your teeth. Even eating may be a challenge. Can you find your mouth? Can you tell what you're eating? What else do you observe? Are you more aware of how things feel, smell, and sound?

Sue wondered if people's walks *sounded* different too. Well, there was one way to find out. She shut her eyes and listened hard.

Click, click, click. There was no doubt what that was—a woman's high heels. The soft padding of the next set of feet told Sue the person was wearing running shoes, but she sneaked a quick peek just to be sure. Then she shut her eyes once more and concentrated on listening. *Clap, slap, clap, slap.* Definitely thongs or backless sandals.

Sue smiled to herself. She was pretty good at this. She listened for the next footsteps. *Squeak,* pause, *squeak,* pause. She frowned. This one was a bit trickier. It was either a very slow walker or a person with one squeaky shoe. But what were the other sounds with it—that rapid *tap, tap, tap* and that trotting *rat-a-tat?*

Unable to figure it out, Sue opened her eyes just as the blind man from the aquarium walked past with his seeing-eye dog. No wonder she hadn't been able to guess. The cane, the shoes, the dog's claws—there were just too many sounds.

The man made his way to the corner and stopped. Then the light changed to green, and a bird began to chirp. Traffic swung into motion once more, and the man and dog started across the intersection.

Sue knew the chirping told the man it was safe to walk, but what she couldn't figure out was how he knew which way to go. If he stepped off the wrong side of the curb, he'd be walking right into the path of oncoming cars!

Sue made a mental note to find out how chirping traffic lights worked. And just so she wouldn't forget, she snapped a picture of the man's retreating back.

Suddenly another sound—a wailing siren—drowned out the traffic signal. Sue swung her head around just as a police cruiser screeched to a halt at the bus stop in front of her. Two uniformed officers slammed out of the car and rushed into the aquarium. ★

22

SOUND EXPERIMENT

Sue discovered she was pretty good at identifying shoe types by the sounds they made. She is an excellent scientist because she stopped, closed her eyes, and listened to the footsteps around her. She was using her observation skills to make hypotheses about what she was hearing. By opening her eyes, she confirmed her hypotheses and drew her conclusion. The steps of a formal experiment in a laboratory are the same as the steps Sue took with her listening.

But Sue might have been surprised to find out that those shoes would have sounded differently if she'd heard them in a stadium or a tunnel. That's because the same sound makes different echoes, depending on its surroundings. Sound travels in waves, and the way waves bounce off objects (echoes/reverberations) and interact with each other (interference) affects how people hear them.

Materials:
* a sound-producing object (e.g., bell, basketball, drum, horn)
* different locations such as a gym, a car interior, a field, a tunnel, a narrow alley, a shower, outdoors beside a large building, a canyon
* a tape recorder

Procedure:
1. Take your sound-producing object (e.g., bell) and tape recorder to one of your chosen locations.
2. Set the recorder up 2 to 2 1/2 metres from where you will ring the bell.
3. Turn on the recorder.
4. Ring the bell.
5. Repeat the preceding three steps for a number of locations.

6. In a quiet room, play back the taped sounds and compare them.
HINT: After each sound, check to make sure it was recorded properly.

What Happened?

The bell rung in a closed bathroom sounded louder than the bell rung in an open field because of your surroundings. When you rang the bell in an open field, some of the sound waves reached your ear, and the rest of the sound waves travelled away across the open field. But when you rang the bell in a closed bathroom, some of the sound waves reached your ear like they did in the field, but something happened to the others travelling away; they reached the wall of the bathroom and bounced back. When sound waves bounce back, they interfere with other sound waves, creating *supercrests* and *supertroughs*. A supercrest is a really big crest that results when two crests meet; they end up combining to form a really big crest. The same thing happens with supertroughs. Since the size of the crest or trough is the sound wave's amplitude, and amplitude determines how loud a sound is, when supercrests and supertroughs reach your ear, the sound is louder than it would be without interference.

More?

To see interference in action, drop objects into a still pool of water at the same time and watch what happens when the resulting waves overlap. If you watch closely, you should be able to see the supercrests and supertroughs.

SOUND

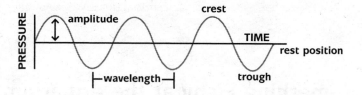

Sound travels in waves, which are composed of crests and troughs. The crest is the highest point of the wave, and the trough the lowest point. The amplitude of a sound wave is the distance between the top of the crest and the rest position (centre line), or the bottom of a trough and the rest position (centre line). This determines its intensity (how loud the sound is). A wavelength (often represented by the Greek symbol lambda: λ) is the distance from one crest to the next crest, or one trough to the next. The wavelength determines the sound's frequency (or pitch: how high or low the sound is). The frequency (represented by f) of a wave is the number of wavelengths per unit of time (number of wavelengths per second). All of these are related in the universal wave equation: $v = f\lambda$, which states that the velocity (or speed) of a wave is equal to the wave's frequency multiplied by its wavelength.

2

Something Fishy at the Aquarium

Fascinated, Sue watched as the police officer yanked open the door of the aquarium, and a wizened old man fell out of it—right into their arms. Gingerly, as if they were handling an ancient mummy, the officers set the man back on his feet.

"Where are you off to in such a hurry, old fella?" one of them asked. He winked at his partner before grinning broadly and adding, "You wouldn't be our robber trying to escape now, would you?"

The man scowled.

"Who're you calling old?" he snapped, pulling himself free. Then he wagged a gnarled finger toward the aquarium and growled, "People have been robbed—lots of people! My wife is one of them. So instead of being a smart aleck, why don't you find out what's going on and arrest someone?"

The smile slid from the officer's face, and he looked as sheepish as a schoolboy who'd been caught cheating on a test. He cleared his throat and touched the brim of his hat. "Yes sir. You're absolutely right. If you'll just come back inside with us, we'll get right on it." He put a hand on the old man's arm and began to steer him toward the door, but the man balked.

"What do you need me for? It was my wife who was robbed!"

The police officer nodded. "We understand. We just need to ask you a few questions. You might have seen something without realizing or perhaps you…"

But that's all Sue caught before the three disappeared inside the aquarium.

With blonde pigtails flying, she hopped off the bench and started after them, but Gina stretched out a hand and yanked her back down.

"Where do you think you're going?"

"Didn't you see that?" Sue demanded.

"See what? The police and the old man go into the aquarium? Yes, of course, I saw that."

"No, no." Sue jumped up again. "Not that." She ran over to a mesh trash container by the aquarium entrance and reached into it. Then she waved a paper in the air. "This! The old man chucked it in here on his way inside."

"What is it?" Nicole asked as she and Gina went to see what Sue was holding.

"It looks like some kind of brochure," Sue replied, turning it over.

Gina pulled a paper out of her purse and shoved it under Sue's nose.

"A brochure like this?" she said.

Sue looked up, surprised. "Yeah. What—"

"It's a schedule of the city's summer events," Gina sighed, "so people can plan their activities. That's how I found out about the endangered exotic shellfish exhibit. It's only going to be here this week. I guess that's why the aquarium is so crowded. Everyone wants to see it." Then she shrugged and waved the schedule at Sue. "So if you were thinking this was some kind of incriminating evidence, forget it. There are thousands of these schedules floating around the city."

But Sue wasn't about to be put off. She tapped a finger on the schedule she'd pulled from the trash. "But this one has different events circled," she said meaningfully. "How do you explain that?"

Gina rolled her eyes. "Simple. The man marked the things that interested him. Why? What do you think they are?"

Caught off guard, Sue stammered, "Uh…I…well…yeah," and then as she gathered her wits again, she added belligerently, "but *why*? That's the real question. Maybe we should investigate."

Gina shook her head and dragged Sue back to the bench.

"Or maybe we should just sit here, mind our own business, and wait for the bus," she said.

"But what if that man *is* a thief?" Sue protested. "Maybe he did rob all those people in the aquarium. Just because he's old, it doesn't mean he can't be a crook."

"Okay, just for the sake of argument, let's say you're right— though why he'd rob his own wife is beyond me. Where's all the stuff he stole?" Gina said. "You saw him. He didn't have anything in his hands," she pointed out logically, "and all he was wearing was a light sport coat. It would be hard to hide anything in that, and anyway, if it had been stuffed with loot, don't you think the police would've noticed?"

"It's not like he was stealing stereo equipment," Sue argued. "He probably just took money—maybe credit cards. And those things

HOLOGRAM

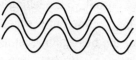

A hologram is created by splitting a laser beam into two beams and recording the results on a photographic plate. Of course, it's a bit more complicated than that, which is probably why banks and credit card companies use holograms as security devices.

To make a hologram, the following things are needed: a laser beam, an object, a lens, and a photographic plate. The object is set up in front of the photographic plate (this acts like film in a camera), and then the laser beam is pointed at it. A beam splitter, set up in front of the beam, divides it into two different beams, which go on either side of the object. Mirrors are carefully placed at different locations around the object to reflect each of the split laser beams back onto the object. A lens is placed in front of each of the split laser beams before they reach the object, so that each laser beam is split into many tiny laser beams. All of these tiny laser beams reflect off the object and onto the photographic plate.

The reason a hologram looks three-dimensional—as if it is jumping out at you—is because all the tiny laser beams are reflecting off the object from different distances, thereby recording the object three-dimensionally on the photographic plate.

would fit into his wallet. And as for his wife, maybe she's in on it too. Maybe they're just pretending she was a victim to avoid suspicion."

But Gina shook her head again. "As usual, you're letting your imagination run away with you. The man threw out a schedule. That's all." She shrugged and looked for the bus again. "Just forget about it and let the police handle things."

"Oh, come on, Gina," Nicole said, taking Sue's side. "Somebody in that aquarium is a thief. And it *could* be that old man. You have to

CRIME SCENE SCIENCE

 Even if the police were certain the old man hadn't committed the robberies inside the aquarium, they couldn't let him leave the crime scene. That's because modern police work isn't just a matter of asking questions and making arrests. These days it involves a careful process of gathering and interpreting evidence in an organized and systematic way, similar to the scientific method. In the scientific method, a scientist tries to prove that A causes B. For example, a scientist may discover that all the children in a certain classroom got sick. She then looks for evidence of what caused the children to get sick. Once she discovers a possible cause for the sickness (maybe the children all ate hamburgers that were not properly cooked) she would try to prove the link between the hamburger and sickness. She would do this by ruling out other possible causes for the sickness. For example, the macaroni salad could have made them

admit he wasn't very happy about going back inside with the police. Aren't you even a little bit curious to find out why?"

"Not really." Gina looked off into the distance again and fanned her face with the brochure she'd pulled out of her purse.

"Sure you are," Sue insisted, jumping in front of her. "Think about it. A robbery has just taken place in this very aquarium, and—"

"Several robberies, actually," Nicole interrupted, sliding into the spot Sue had just vacated.

sick, but only two children ate the salad. The only food that all the children ate was the hamburger. Therefore, the hamburger would be the most likely cause of the sickness.

Similarly, police try to prove that a suspect committed a crime. Police have to make sure the evidence can be directly linked to the crime scene and suspect. They try to rule out other explanations for who committed the crime and how and why it was committed. (In science these other explanations are called alternate hypotheses.) Police are highly trained in gathering crime-scene evidence and asking revealing questions that will provide forensic scientists with important clues. Insects, fibres, fingerprints, body fluids, shards of glass, and even scraps of paper may at first seem unimportant, but upon closer examination in a lab they could prove to be the evidence that solves a crime.

"Right," Sue nodded. "Several robberies and we were here when they happened. We probably walked right by the thief. Heck, we could've seen the crook in action and not even realized it." She waved her camera in the air. "Who knows—I might even have caught the robberies on film! And you want us to believe you're not curious?"

Gina shook her head. "I'm not."

"Not at all?"

"Not at all."

"You really don't care?"

Gina stood up and, peering over Sue's head, pointed down the street toward an approaching bus.

"Right now all I care about is getting on that bus. Come on. Let's go."

Sue would have liked to protest further, but there didn't seem much point. Gina was past listening. She sent the older girl her best glare, but Gina was too busy digging through her purse to notice. Tissues, hair pick, lipstick, pen, notepad, chewing gum—one by one, she hauled each item out of her purse. Then she slid the purse from her shoulder and began digging through it with both hands. When the bus pulled into the stop and its door opened, Gina was still rummaging through the purse. Her forehead had become creased with concern.

"Are ya getting on, or aren't ya?" the driver called impatiently.

Gina looked up and stared blankly at him, and that's when Sue realized something was wrong.

The driver waited a few more seconds, then slammed the door shut and merged into the traffic once more.

Sue touched Gina's arm.

"What's the matter?" And then when there was no response, she tried again. "Gina?"

This time Sue's voice made it through the fog surrounding the older girl, and a look of amazement spread across Gina's face.

"My wallet's gone," she said, as if she didn't believe it herself. "I've been robbed."

"Not you too!" Sue gasped.

"Did you have much money?" Nicole asked anxiously.

Gina tried to remember. "About ten dollars, I think." Then a worried look took over her face. "But my parents' credit card was in my wallet too. Mom gave it to me this morning to get some new jeans. I'll have to call her right away so she can cancel it." Gina groaned.

"There was other stuff too. None of it would be worth anything to a thief, but it is to me." Her face contorted painfully as she recalled the contents of her stolen wallet. "I had so many pictures! And my social insurance card was in there too, and my discount card for the music store, and…and…"

With each new recollection, the expression on Gina's face became fiercer. Finally she exclaimed, "My CAGIS membership card was in that wallet!" and she turned and began marching back toward the aquarium entrance.

"Where are you going?" Nicole said.

Gina whirled around. "To catch the crook who stole it!"

There was a second's pause before Sue called after her. "Need any help?" ★

EVIDENCE EXPERIMENT

Would you be a good crime investigator? Are you observant? Would you recognize a clue? Would you know why something was evidence? Would you know what questions to ask?

Create your own crime scene to find out.

Materials:

* a crime scene (actually, any scene will do—a kitchen, a sundeck, a playground, a car)
* a magnifying glass
* a pencil/pen and notebook
* several plastic bags to put evidence in
* witnesses, if there are any

Procedure:

The purpose of your investigation is to find out as much as you can about a specific place so you can make reasonable guesses about who has recently been there and what they were doing.

1. Check out all the clues and use your five senses to observe. Clues might be cigarette butts, ashes in a fireplace, the contents of a glass, lipstick on a tissue, a particular odour, footprints in the carpet, animal hair, cookie crumbs, etc.
2. Place each piece of evidence in a plastic bag and note where each was found, as well as other relevant information.
3. If there are people in the room, ask them questions and note their responses in your notebook.
4. Review your evidence and form conclusions about who has recently been at the scene.

What Happened?

What sorts of evidence did you find? Did the witnesses' testimony agree with your evidence? What evidence could be misinterpreted? What statements can you make with absolute certainty about the crime scene and who has been there?

Crime investigation, like the scientific method, uses the five senses to observe and make hypotheses, based on careful observation. Through the process of elimination, the crime investigator and scientist determine which hypothesis fits the evidence best.

More?
Take fingerprints of friends and family members. Are the fingerprints of family members more alike than the fingerprints of your friends?

3

Now You See it—Now You Don't

The following day, the three girls gathered around the kitchen table at Nicole's house to discuss the thefts.

"Six robberies in half an hour." Sue did some quick calculations in her head. "Wow! That's one robbery every five minutes! The crook couldn't have done much better if he'd had his victims hand over their wallets at the door."

"Actually, only four wallets were taken," Gina pointed out. "Four wallets, a purse, and a gold watch. And the police got all of them back. They were in the aquarium trash containers."

"All except the watch," Nicole reminded her.

"And the money," Sue added. "Don't forget that. The crook made off with nearly $900."

"Well, look on the bright side," Nicole said. "He didn't take any credit cards or personal stuff. Right, Gina?"

"Pardon?" Gina looked up from her wallet. After keeping it overnight and dusting it for fingerprints, the police had allowed her to have it back, and now she was checking its contents. "Oh, right... I think." Then she frowned.

"What's the matter?" Nicole asked.

"Well," the older girl began, "no matter how many times I go over it, I can't think of a single minute when the thief could have taken my wallet. It was in my purse, and my purse was hanging from my shoulder. And I'm absolutely positive I never put it down—not even for a second. Don't you think I would have noticed if someone had stuck a hand into it?"

"That old guy was obviously a professional," Nicole said.

"And that's another thing," Gina went on. "I never even saw that man before he bolted out of the aquarium."

Nicole raised an eyebrow. "You weren't supposed to. That's what makes him a professional."

Gina shrugged and sighed. "I guess."

"Maybe my photographs will tell us something," Sue suggested.

Gina frowned. "And that's another thing. I still think you should have given the police your film."

Sue waved away her friend's concern. "Until we know for sure that we have something here, what would be the point?"

"I guess," Gina conceded. "When will you get the pictures back?"

Sue glanced at the clock on the wall. "My mom is grocery shopping right now. She said she'd pick them up and drop them off here on her way home."

As if on cue, the doorbell rang, and Nicole's golden lab, Darby, who'd been snoozing under the table, sprang to his feet and began to bark. The three girls jumped out of their chairs and raced after him down the hall.

When the front door flew open, spilling the laughing girls and barking dog onto the porch, Sue's mother fell back a couple of steps and threw up her arms.

"Stop! I give up. Take the pictures, but spare my life."

Sue rolled her eyes as she took the envelope of photographs from her mother's outstretched hand.

"You are too funny, Mother," she said.

Mrs. Watson grinned. "I thought so." Then her expression became more serious. "I hope you girls aren't tearing the place apart in there. Mr. and Mrs. Burke won't be too happy if their house is in ruins when they get home from work."

Nicole scratched the dog's ears and smiled. "Don't worry. Everything's fine. The doorbell just set Darby off. You caught him napping, and now he's embarrassed that he didn't hear you coming. The barking is just a cover-up."

As if he knew he was being talked about, Darby whined and his ears drooped.

Everyone laughed, and then Mrs. Watson started back down the stairs.

"Well, enjoy the afternoon, girls. And, Sue, please be home in time to help me get supper. Bye now."

As soon as they'd closed the door, the girls tore back into the kitchen and spread the pictures onto the table. Then bunching together, they pored over them, searching for something incriminating.

"Wow! Look at this!" Sue gasped, stabbing one of the photographs with her finger.

Nicole and Gina immediately swarmed in closer to examine the picture Sue was pointing at.

"I must be blind," Nicole shrugged, twisting a springy black curl around her finger, "but I don't know what it is we're supposed to be looking at."

PHOTOGRAPHY AND THE CAMERA

The word photography comes from two Greek words meaning light and writing, an appropriate choice since the process of photography involves two procedures: the accurate capture (writing) of a real image and the permanent recording of that image through the use of light.

We use a camera to form and record an image (picture) onto film. The camera works just like the eye (see p. 18). The image passing through the camera or eye lens is inverted, and an upside-down image is formed on the film (or retina). The film, like the retina, captures the light, which produces an image. The aperture of the camera is the hole through which light passes. This aperture is like the pupil of the eye. The lens of a camera (like the lens of an eye) is convex and focuses the light onto the film. The film areas hit by light go through a chemical reaction. Then, when the film is developed, it goes through another series of chemical reactions, which produces a photograph.

"It's the picture I took of you and the dolphin," Sue explained.

"That's obvious," Gina said. "The question is—what does it have to do with the robbery?"

Sue shrugged. "Nothing. But it's a really good picture, don't you think? There's not even any glare on the glass from my flash."

Gina growled impatiently, "Could we discuss your wonderful photography some other time? Right now, I'd like to find the crook who stole my wallet."

"Right," Sue said. "Sorry."

"Hey, I know," Nicole piped up, her brown cheeks turning into round balls as her mouth parted in a huge white grin. "Why don't we sort the pictures into groups? We could put the ones that show the animals in the exhibits in one pile and the ones with people in the other. I have a feeling that might speed things up."

"Good idea," Gina agreed. "Sue, you've snapped some pictures of the victims too. Maybe we should put all those photographs in their own pile. Who knows? There might be some sort of pattern."

"Right," the other two agreed, and the girls quickly got to work.

In no time, the pictures were divided into groups, and as Nicole and Gina examined the ones containing people, Sue sifted through the ones of the animal exhibits.

Although she went through them carefully three times, she couldn't find a single clue. All she had was a stack of fish photographs. And if she was being really honest, she had to admit that most of them weren't even all that good. Unlike the photograph of the dolphin, most of the pictures taken through the aquarium windows were marred by the camera's flash. Not only was there a starburst glare in each one, but Sue's reflection in the window made the pictures look like double exposures.

Sue sighed and stared dejectedly at the photograph in her hand. She was so sure the snapshots were going to provide a lead.

But they hadn't—unless Gina and Nicole had found something, that is.

Sue tossed down the photograph and was about to turn to her friends when the strangest thing happened. As her mind relaxed and her gaze became blurred, the tropical fish in the snapshot receded, and the reflection in the glass popped into focus instead. Without meaning to, Sue had taken a picture of what was going on in the aquarium behind her!

With renewed hope, she began flipping through the photographs again.

And then she found it.

"Look at this!" she said, waving one of the pictures at Nicole and Gina. Immediately the other girls stopped their own search and gave Sue their full attention.

"Did you find something?" Nicole asked hopefully.

Sue beamed. "You bet I did. Take a look at this."

Gina and Nicole squinted at the photograph.

"I don't see anything but fish," Gina said.

"No, no." Sue shook her head. "Don't look at that. Look at the reflection."

"What reflection?"

"In the window. Look at what's reflected in the window."

"Oh, yeah," Nicole said, suddenly seeing the picture within the picture. "You can see the people behind you. I think I see the old man who ran out of the aquarium. And there's another man beside him."

"Let me see that." Gina snatched the picture away and peered hard at it. "Okay, fine," she said, when she'd had a closer look. "So the old man is standing with a bunch of people. So what? He isn't doing anything suspicious. The only thing your picture proves is that someone was feeding the blind man's dog."

Nicole frowned. "What are you talking about?"

Gina handed her the picture.

"Ah, now I see," Nicole said. "The dog has something in its mouth."

"Yeah," Sue said smugly. "But I don't think it's food. Look closer."

"You're right," Nicole agreed. "It looks like he's carrying some-

REFLECTED LIGHT

Though Sue thought she was taking a picture of the fish in the aquarium, she ended up photographing what was happening behind her as well.

How was that possible?

Let's just say it was a trick with mirrors—well, sort of. At any rate, the window was acting like a mirror. The people behind Sue were reflected in the glass, and Sue simply photographed them.

Like sound, light acts like waves, which have certain frequencies and wavelengths and are commonly called rays. Regular reflection happens when parallel light rays bounce off a flat, smooth, polished surface like a mirror or window and remain parallel even after bouncing off the surface. The light ray is called the *incident* ray before it reaches the mirror, and the *reflected* ray after it bounces off the mirror. When a light ray is reflected off a mirror, the angle of incidence is equal to the angle of reflection. That means that the light ray leaves the mirror (angle b) at the same angle as it originally hit the mirror (angle a).

thing." She put the snapshot down and rubbed her eyes. "The question is *what?* That picture is just too busy and small to tell."

"What we need is a magnifying glass," Sue suggested.

"That might help," Gina agreed. "Or we could just go over to my house and I'll enlarge the picture on my computer." ✦

However, in Sue's photographs, not all the light rays were reflected. When light rays strike a mirror, all the rays are reflected, so a photograph taken into a mirror clearly reflects the scene behind it. With glass, however, some of the rays are able to get through. As a result, the camera picked up the fish on the other side of the window as well as the reflections in the window, giving Sue's photographs the appearance of double exposures.

Incident ray

a

a=b   Mirror

b

Reflected ray

FINGERPRINT EXPERIMENT

The police took Gina's wallet because it was crime evidence. Otherwise, the Science Squad could have dusted it for fingerprints themselves.

Fingerprints are formed before we are born and stay with us all our lives. And though there are well over six billion people in the world, no two sets of fingerprints are exactly alike! It is this uniqueness that has made fingerprinting a reliable and widely used crime-solving tool.

Leaving our fingerprints behind is easy. We do it every time we handle something. The natural oils in our skin automatically imprint the grooves and ridges of our fingertips onto any objects we touch.

Lifting fingerprints off objects is a bit more work, but not difficult to do. See if you can identify people from the prints they leave behind.

Materials:
* identical, clear, smooth, drinking glasses
* pens or pencils
* pieces of white and black paper
* fine paintbrushes
* talcum powder
* clear cellophane tape
* stamp pad

Procedure
1. Wash and dry as many identical glasses as there are people taking part in the experiment. Be sure NOT to get your fingerprints on the glasses.
2. Give each person a glass and a square of paper with a number written on it. Have each person tape his or her square of paper

to the bottom of the glass so that the number cannot be seen. Ask them to touch ONLY their own glass with their bare hands so that only one set of fingerprints is left on each glass.

3. Without getting any more fingerprints on any of the glasses, mix them up so no one knows which is which. Then inside each glass, place a square of paper with a letter on it.

4. With the paintbrushes, lightly dust talcum powder over the surface of the glasses. Gently blow the excess powder away. The powder on the fingerprints should stay. Carefully brush the powder spots until the fingerprint appears. (You might want to try this technique ahead of time to perfect it.)

5. Press a piece of cellophane tape over the fingerprint and peel it off the glass. Stick the tape onto a piece of black paper to see it better.

6. Beside the fingerprint, write the letter of the glass from which the print was taken.

7. When this has been done for each glass, use the stamp pad and the white paper to get fingerprints of everyone taking part in the experiment. Have each person write their name and the number they taped to the bottom of the glass on the paper with their fingerprints.

8. Compare the fingerprints lifted from each glass to the fingerprint samples. Can you match each person to the glass she touched?

What Happened?

There are three types of fingerprint patterns: arches move upward in the centre in an arch shape; loops flow either in the direction of the little finger or thumb; and whorls are circular.

Were you able to trace the owner of the fingerprints left on each glass? What differences did you notice in each person's finger-prints? Did you notice lines that looked like arches? How about loops? Did you see any whorls? Were they different sizes or in different locations? The fingerprints lifted from each glass should match the fingerprints of the person who held the glass.

Police officers and forensic scientists often use the fingerprint technique to identify suspects and match suspects to different clues. For example, a forensic scientist would search a murder weapon for prints to find out who used the weapon to commit the murder.

$\sqrt{225}$ NaCl H_2O $A^2 + B^2 = C^2$ CO_2

0010
1010
0100
1100
1011
1000
0101
1110
0110
0001

4

Partners in Crime

Sue and Nicole hovered over Gina's shoulder as she worked.

"So this is a scanner," Sue said, watching Gina position the photograph on the glass surface. "It looks like a photocopier to me."

Gina nodded. "That's because it's a flatbed scanner. But there are lots of other kinds too—hand-held ones, sheet-fed scanners, and even drum scanners." She shrugged. "They all look different, and they all run a bit differently, but basically they do the same thing—they change a hard copy of something into a form that can be used on the computer." Gina gestured to the reproduction of the photograph on the monitor and grinned. "Voila."

Sue squinted at the screen.

"Okay, so we've got the photograph on computer. Now what?"

Gina's fingers started to fly over the keyboard. "Now we use an image-editing program to find out what the picture is hiding."

Sue watched with fascination as Gina expertly zoomed into the background of the photograph, making it lighter, cutting away the unneeded parts, and enlarging the rest.

Little by little, the snapshot that had been almost impossible to see before gave up its secrets and not only could all three girls see the face of the man patting the dog, they could also make out what the dog had in its mouth.

Nicole gasped and grabbed Gina's shoulder, causing the other girl to jump out of her chair. "Do you see that?" she gulped. "It's…it's …it's…"

Gina nodded and sank slowly back into her chair. "You're right. It is."

Sue's eyes grew wide and her hand flew up to her mouth. "But then…then…that means…"

Gina nodded again. "Uh-huh."

Sue grabbed the pile of photographs off the computer desk and began rummaging through them.

"What're you doing?" Gina asked.

"I have a hunch this isn't just a coincidence," Sue replied, shoving a pile of pictures into each of the other girls' hands.

Gina frowned. "What are we supposed to do with these?"

"Find all the pictures with the dog and the blind man."

Five minutes later the three girls huddled around Gina's computer in stunned silence.

"Wow!" It was Sue who broke the silence. "If I wasn't seeing this with my own eyes, I never would've believed it."

"Me neither," Nicole agreed. "But pictures don't lie. That dog definitely has a gold watch in its mouth. There's no doubt about it." She nudged Sue with her elbow. "It looks like we were wrong about that old man being the thief. All along it was Rover here. Your photograph caught him red-handed—I mean, red-pawed."

Sue groaned and gave Nicole a hip check.

"Wait a second," Gina frowned. "We're jumping to conclusions here. How do we know the dog didn't just pick the watch up off the floor? Think about it—a dog as a pickpocket? Besides, I never even saw that animal until I crashed into the blind guy, and even then, the dog wasn't anywhere near me. So how could it have stolen my wallet?"

Sue shook her head. "I don't think it did." She took a deep breath. It was time to elaborate on the rest of her theory. The question was would her friends believe her.

"What?" Nicole's eyebrows knotted together when Sue had finished. "Now you have me totally confused. First you say the dog is the crook, and now you say it isn't."

Sue shook her head again. "No, that's not what I'm saying. The dog is our crook all right—at least, he's one of them."

"What do you mean?" Gina's eyes narrowed suspiciously.

Sue wagged a finger at the computer screen. "Scan another picture of the dog and people." When Gina brought one up onto the monitor, Sue pointed to a figure in the background and said, "Now look. You see that? That's another one of the victims—right? And look who's standing beside him."

"It's the blind man," Gina said. "So?"

Sue told Gina to scan another photograph, and when she did, Sue again pointed to one of the people in it. "Another victim." Then she gestured to another person, and said smugly, "and guess who's walking away from her."

"It's that blind guy again!" Nicole exclaimed, her black eyes becoming almost round. "He's the other thief. And you ran right into him, Gina! That's when he must've robbed you."

But Gina looked unconvinced. "Are you trying to tell me that a blind man and a seeing-eye dog are responsible for all those thefts?" She shook her head. "No. It's just not possible."

PAVLOV AND CLASSICAL CONDITIONING

At one time or another, most of us have tried to teach a dog to do something—to sit, fetch, beg, roll over, or shake a paw. To let the dog know it's doing the right thing, we reward it with a treat, and the dog soon learns that offering its paw will result in a dog cookie. This type of training is called operant conditioning because we *operate* upon our environment. It means that when we are rewarded for behaviour we continue doing it, and when we are punished for behaviour we stop doing it.

There is another type of learning even more basic than using rewards or punishments. Back in the 1920s, a Russian Nobel Prize–winning physiologist named Ivan Pavlov discovered this other type of learning, which has become known as classical conditioning. Pavlov was studying the digestive system and was examining the amount of saliva dogs produced when food was in their mouths. However, Pavlov observed something unexpected (this often happens in science) that led to a new discovery. He noticed that the dogs began to salivate when food was put in front of them, even *before* they began to eat. This was interesting because normally it is the food in the mouth that *causes* the salivation. Yet the dogs salivated just seeing the food. The dogs weren't taught to salivate; salivation was a natural physical response to the stimulus of food. In scientific terms, we refer to this as an unconditioned response to unconditioned stimulus, with the unconditioned response being the salivation and the unconditioned stimulus being the food.

Pavlov then wondered if he could make the dogs salivate when presented with something totally unrelated to food, such as a bell. Pavlov noted that when he rang a bell,* the dogs did not salivate. There was no relation at all between the sound of a bell and salivation.

Next, Pavlov began ringing the bell each time he offered the dogs food, and as you might expect, the dogs salivated. He did this repeatedly over a lengthy period of time.

But it is what Pavlov did next that proved his theory. He rang the bell without offering the dogs any food, and, as he had hypothesized, the animals began to salivate. He had managed to get the dogs to associate the ringing of the bell with food, and, as a result, the dogs began to salivate at the sound of the bell, even though there was no food. Through association he had created a relationship between two unconnected things. Salivation had become a conditioned response to a conditioned stimulus (the bell).

For more information on reflexes and conditioning, see: **http://www.101_dog_training_tips.com/Behavior/Foundation _Of_Training.shtml**

Some people argue that Pavlov used a light, not a bell, in his experiments, but it doesn't change the results.

Sue couldn't believe Gina was being so stubborn. "Why not? Who has a better sense of touch than a blind person?"

"It all happened too fast," Gina argued. "The whole incident couldn't have taken more than a few seconds. How could he possibly get my wallet that quickly? And why didn't I notice anything?"

"Because you weren't supposed to. He took your attention away from what he was doing. You were so busy worrying about the collision that you weren't tuned in to anything else," Sue explained logically.

"That's right," Nicole agreed. "It's kind of like legerdemain."

"Ledger *who*?" Sue demanded.

"Sleight of hand," Nicole explained. "You know—magic! Everybody knows magic isn't real. It's just tricks. People are only fooled because magicians get them paying attention to the wrong stuff while they pull their tricks."

Gina's face relaxed and she nodded. "Good point."

Sue sensed the older girl's resistance was weakening. It was time to hit her with another fact. Sue rummaged through the pile of photographs until she found the one of the dog holding the watch. She pushed it under Gina's nose.

"Do you notice anything unusual about this picture *besides* the watch in the dog's mouth?"

Nicole and Gina squinted at the photograph for several seconds, but eventually shook their heads.

Sue couldn't keep the smile off her face as she said, "Well, the dog is in the picture, but there's no sign of the blind man. Doesn't it seem a bit strange that he and his seeing-eye dog aren't together?"

"You're right!" Nicole gasped. "And that would explain how there could be so many robberies in such a short time."

There was a pause as the girls thought about the situation.

At last Gina sighed. "Okay. I have to admit it makes sense. But how do we find out for sure?"

Sue's grin got bigger and her blue eyes started to dance. "It just so happens, I have an idea."

• • •

While Gina approached the receptionist at the Canadian National Institute for the Blind, Sue and Nicole sat down in the waiting area. Too excited to stay still more than two minutes, Sue got up again, wandered over to a nearby book rack, and picked up one of the hardcover novels. But when she opened it, she discovered it had no words—just page after page of bumps, as if someone had poked all of them with a pin. The book was written in Braille. Sue closed her eyes and ran her fingers lightly over the perforations. Of course, she didn't know the Braille alphabet, but even so, she couldn't tell one bump from another.

She tried to detect some sort of pattern to the bumps, but she kept getting distracted by the sounds around her. She could hear Nicole turning the pages of a magazine, and she could pick up snatches of music from a radio somewhere. She could even catch bits and pieces of Gina's conversation with the receptionist.

"He said he would be happy to come to one of our CAGIS meetings and talk to us about how scientific advances have made life easier for the blind. The only problem is I've lost the paper with his name. All I have is this picture." Sue knew Gina was showing the receptionist the photograph of the blind man and his dog at the traffic light.

She smiled. Who would've thought Gina was such a good liar?

Then another sound caught Sue's attention. It was a squeak. *Squeak*, pause, *squeak*, pause, *squeak*, pause. She cocked her head to one side and listened harder. Now where had she heard that sound before? She glanced around the room, and then, in shock, nearly dropped the book.

53

It was the blind guy! He was barely a metre away from her—there was no way she could be mistaken. It was him all right—except he wasn't wearing sunglasses, and he had no seeing-eye dog with him.

THE BRAIN

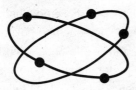

Though Sue could feel the raised bumps of the Braille writing, she wasn't able to distinguish one set of bulges from another. That's because her brain wasn't trained to be sensitive to them.

The brain is the central part of the human nervous system, the part of the body that determines how people experience the world. It controls such things as emotions, thoughts, sensations, movement, language, and memory. The nervous system contains nerve cells called neurons, whose job it is to receive nerve impulses and send them to other parts of the body. Though all human brains have the same basic structure, the way neurons develop and connect with other neurons changes from person to person. That's because different backgrounds and experiences cause each individual's brain parts to develop differently.

A baby is born with a brain only 23 percent the size of an adult brain. At the age of two, the child's brain is 75 percent of its adult size. The child's brain does not grow continuously but

He wasn't blind at all!

Unable to move, Sue watched him stride across the room, move a peg on a wall board to the "OUT" position, and then push open the heavy glass door and leave.

has growth spurts, beginning around two years old and continuing at 6, 10, and 14 years old. Each spurt makes the brain 10 percent heavier than it was before. When a baby is born, it has all the neurons it will ever have. The neurons keep making new connections to other neurons called synapses, but they also take away unneeded connections. After age two the brain is pruning (removing) many synapses (like pruning some branches of a tree) to remove unneeded connections.

Some scientists speculate that Albert Einstein's genius for math may have been because he had more neural connections in the math part of the brain than other people. For more information, see Einstein on p. 100 .

Take Sue's experience with the Braille book. Though her fingers accessed the same area of the brain as a blind person's fingers would, Sue's brain doesn't have as many neural connections to sense and understand the Braille letters and consequently that particular area isn't as dense. For more information on neurons, see p. 103.

Sue looked over at Nicole on the waiting room sofa. Her nose was buried deep in the pages of the magazine. Obviously, she hadn't noticed a thing. And Gina was still talking to the receptionist, so she wouldn't have seen the man either.

Like a robot, Sue made her way to the door and peered out the glass. The man had already disappeared. Then she glanced up at the IN/OUT board. Finally she headed toward Gina.

"With only the man's back showing, it's difficult to say for certain who it is," the receptionist was telling Gina. "It could be almost anyone. But if it's a speaker you're looking for, I'm sure there are all kinds of people who would be happy to talk to your CAGIS organization."

"Excuse me," Sue cut in, when the woman paused. "I'm sorry to interrupt, but does a Mike Crosby work here?"

The receptionist smiled. "Yes—and no. He works out of this branch, though he isn't here often."

Sue and Gina exchanged puzzled looks.

The receptionist smiled again.

"He's one of our dog trainers." ✶

BRAIN EXPERIMENT

Try this cool experiment called "The Stroop Effect," named after J. Ridley Stroop, the person who discovered it. Stroop was a psychologist in the 1930s. He discovered this effect and used it for his Ph.D. thesis in psychology (a Ph.D. thesis is a very long report a university student has to do to get a degree called "Doctor of Philosophy" or Ph.D. for short).

Materials:
- ❋ a large sheet of paper
- ❋ six different coloured markers

Procedure:
1. Make up a chart of the words green, red, purple, blue, orange, and white. Write each word in a coloured marker that is *not* the colour of the word you are writing. For instance, write green in orange marker, red in blue marker, etc.
2. Now look at the chart you've drawn, and say the *colour* of each word out loud. *Do not read* the words; just say their colours.
3. Now, gather together some people of different ages, like a parent, a friend, and a younger sibling.
4. Have each of them do the Stroop test, and time how long it takes them to name all of the colours correctly.
5. Record the times for each person.
6. Who was the fastest? Who was the slowest? Was there any connection between the age of the person and the amount of time it took them to name the colours?

What Happened?
Your brain got confused! Most people start by naming the first two colours, then start laughing as their brains seize up with confusion.

The problem is your brain is programmed to read. When you're presented with the task of reading the names of colours, your brain has no problem. But when it has to name the colours of the words, your brain wants to read the words rather than name the colours.

Usually, younger children have an easier time with the test than older children and adults. Can you figure out why?

Younger children's brains aren't as good at reading as yours or your parents' brains so they don't have the same urge to read the words. Therefore they're able to name the colours more easily.

5

Stakeout

"Now we go to the police," Gina said emphatically once the Science Squad had left the CNIB. "We tell them what we've found out, give them the photographs, and let them do the rest."

Sue's mouth dropped open.

"You're kidding—right?" she said, though the look on Gina's face definitely implied she wasn't. "If we go to the police with the measly evidence we have right now, all they're going to do is laugh at us. Think about it. It was hard enough getting *you* to believe Crosby was the thief. So why would the police? If we had a picture of him with his hand in somebody's pocket, that would be different —but we don't."

Gina rolled her eyes. "So what are you suggesting? That we get one?"

When Sue didn't answer, Gina took a step backward and shook her head.

"Oh, no," she moaned. "Please tell me you're not thinking what I think you're thinking."

● ● ●

"I can't believe I let you talk me into this," Gina grumbled, peering around the barnlike room. It was already crowded with people. "This place is a zoo. What makes you think Crosby will show up *here*?"

"For exactly the reason you just said—it's a zoo. Well…an antique auction actually, but it amounts to the same thing—lots of people standing around with lots of money in their wallets. It's the perfect opportunity for a pickpocket. And just like the aquarium, it was listed on that schedule of summer events. The write-up said it was going to have the largest selection of collectors' pieces the city has ever seen. I bet you anything Crosby will be here."

Gina looked unconvinced, so Sue continued. "You have to think positive, Gina. But even if he doesn't show up, we'll still get him. It's just a matter of time. In the meanwhile, we're at an auction. So why not enjoy ourselves? Look at all the cool stuff there is. You're the expert on old things—this has got to be like a toy store for you." Sue checked her watch. "The bidding doesn't start for half an hour. Let's look around. Nicole is keeping watch at the entrance. She'll call us on your cell if Crosby shows up."

Gina let out an enormous sigh and closed her eyes. "Why do I let you talk me into these things?"

Sue grinned and grabbed her friend's hand. "You love it, and you know it. Come on."

Squeezing through the crush of bodies, the girls moved from display to display, admiring the hundreds of items for sale. At first, the auction hall reminded Sue of a furniture warehouse. Everywhere they turned there were tables, cabinets, chairs, mirrors, dressers, and sofas in every style and size imaginable. The other browsers commented knowledgeably about the history and craftsmanship of each piece, and Sue's ears were soon burning from the nonstop flow of information.

Ornately framed oil paintings of hunting dogs, horses, and rolling countryside stared at Sue and Gina from easels, and the girls found themselves flipping through their programs to learn the age, artist, previous owners, and characteristics of each piece of art.

Everything seemed to be for sale—silver trays and teapots, fragile china, jewellery, ornaments and vases, tools, leather-bound books, and even farm machinery. Despite the wide assortment, the items all had one thing in common. They were very, very old.

"Look at this," Sue said as she admired what appeared to be a miniature pair of binoculars. The tag attached read Lot #327. She checked her program. "Opera glasses," she read aloud. "Cool."

When she got no response, she glanced around. Gina wasn't there. Sue peered past the people beside her and spied Gina two tables away. She called her name, but the other girl was so absorbed in whatever was on the table that she didn't hear. Sue sighed and began working her way back through the mob.

"Now I know what a spawning salmon must feel like," she muttered as she fought against the flow of bodies.

"Didn't you hear me calling you?" she said when she finally reached Gina's side.

"Huh?" Gina mumbled absently. And then without waiting for Sue to repeat her question, she said, "This is fantastic!"

"What is?" Sue turned her attention to the table.

Gina gestured to one of the objects on it.

Sue scratched her head as she eyed the mound of metal her friend was pointing to. "Okay, I'll bite. What is it?"

CELLPHONES

A recent television commercial shows a woman using her cellphone to buy a soft drink from a machine. It seems far-fetched, but according to experts in cellphone technology, that might soon be quite common. Cellphones are able to do more and more all the time. They allow users not only to phone from anywhere but to fax and check their e-mail as well. Some cellphones are equipped with GPS (Global Positioning Systems), which is like having a built-in map in your telephone. And it's predicted that soon users will even be able to access their debit cards through their cellphones.

Do you realize what that means? It means that you'll be able to order pizza on a crowded beach, pay for it over the phone, and have the delivery person locate you through the GPS while you walk along the sandbar. Wow!

"A dumpy level." The awe in Gina's voice was unmistakable.

"Well, it's a dumpy something." Sue frowned harder at what looked like a stubby brass telescope. "What the heck is a dumpy level?"

"It's a surveying tool," Gina replied. "Archaeologists use them for setting up the grids at dig sites. And according to the program here, this dumpy level belonged to one of the scientists of the Leakey expedition at the Olduvai Gorge in Africa."

"*Leaky* expedition? *Dumpy* level? Archaeology isn't one of the more precise sciences, is it?" Sue observed sarcastically.

Gina gave her a shove. "Not that kind of leaky, you goof. Louis and Mary Leakey were famous archaeologists who discovered *Homo habilis*. And believe me, that was pretty major because *Homo habilis* is considered to be the first real toolmaker and the first true ancestor of humans."

Sue eyed Gina skeptically. "How can scientists tell all that from a bunch of bones? And how do they even know that the skeletons they find weren't buried by some murderer trying to hide the evidence of his crime?"

"Because they can scientifically verify the age of the bones and artifacts they find."

"How?"

But before Gina could reply, her cellphone jangled in her purse. Quickly, she pulled it out, switched it on, and put it up to her ear.

"Hello." She frowned and covered her other ear in an effort to block out the noise. "Sorry. Say that again." Then suddenly she was scanning the room, trying to see over the heads of the people around her. "Where? Uh-huh. Okay, we're on it." There was a pause. Then Gina nodded and said, "Good idea. Talk to you later."

Gina switched off the phone and turned to Sue. She took a deep breath.

"I hate to admit it, but it looks like you were right. He's here. Get your camera ready."

But before she could go into details, the high-pitched squeal of microphone feedback interrupted her, and a deep male voice filled the air.

"Ladies and gentlemen, the auction will commence in five minutes. I repeat—five minutes. Please assemble in the open area near the main entrance. Thank you."

Instantly the tide of people began moving toward the auction block, and the girls were swept along in the swell, jostled and bumped with every step.

"Man," Sue grumbled to Gina, "it's wall to wall people in here. I bet even *I* could lift someone's wallet in this place."

Gina responded by hugging her purse closer.

As the girls got nearer the auction area, they spied Nicole standing at the entrance. She nodded toward the left side of the bidding floor. Immediately both Sue and Gina squinted in that direction. Then Gina elbowed Sue and pointed.

"Over there. See him?"

Dressed in a camel-coloured sport coat and brown slacks, Mike Crosby was practically invisible among all the other people. If it weren't for his sunglasses, Sue would never have noticed him.

"Yup, I got him," she replied, getting her video camera ready. "But we're going to have to get closer if I'm going to get anything incriminating."

That was easier said than done. The bidders had all claimed their pieces of floor and weren't anxious to relinquish any ground to the two girls pushing through the crowd. Nevertheless, Sue forged ahead, ignoring the dirty looks from the people she passed, while Gina trailed after her with an apologetic smile pasted onto her face.

They were about five feet away from Mike Crosby when the bidding started.

"Lots one through five are offered as a set," the auctioneer said. "Tiffany earrings, bracelet, ring, necklace, and brooch from the collection of the late Mrs. Davenport-Jenkins. Diamonds and blue sapphires set in 18-karat gold. We'll open the bidding at..."

The auctioneer spoke faster than Sue could listen, and she wondered how anyone could understand what he was saying. She also wondered how people were bidding. The only one talking was the auctioneer, but the cost of the items being sold kept going up.

"Whatever you do, don't raise your hand or nod your head," Gina mumbled into her ear, "or you'll have bought something. And at the prices things are going for, I'm pretty sure you can't afford it."

But the other people in the crowd obviously could, and that reminded Sue to concentrate on Mike Crosby and his dog. If they didn't stop him, he was going to make off with a fortune.

He didn't make them wait long. With one sideways step, he casually bumped into the person standing next to him. Even though Sue was watching for it, she almost missed him pick the man's pocket. She certainly didn't catch it on video. It was over before she even got the camera turned on.

"Did you get that?" Gina whispered.

"No," Sue whispered back. "He was too fast."

She was obviously going to have to keep her camera trained on him the whole time and just pray he didn't notice her.

With his dog at his side, Mike Crosby shuffled sideways again and bumped into the next person. This time Sue was ready and shot the whole thing, including Crosby's hand in the man's back pocket.

Apologizing, he moved again and then again, and each time he lifted someone's wallet, Sue caught him on video.

She turned excitedly to Gina. "We've got him. If this video turns out, we'll have all the evidence we need."

Crosby was slowly working his way to the exit—picking pockets as he went, and though Sue had put her video camera away, she and Gina followed him.

Nicole was still standing beside the door, and just as Crosby passed her, two police officers appeared from nowhere and, placing their hands firmly on Crosby's arms and saying something quietly into his ear, they led him away to a nearby room and closed the door.

When Gina and Sue reached Nicole, she was grinning like a cat that had swallowed a canary.

"Where did those policemen come from?" Sue asked in amazement.

Nicole's grin got bigger than ever. "They've been here the whole time." She shrugged. "I didn't think it could hurt to have a backup.

And when I called Gina on her cell, she agreed with me. The police didn't believe me at first, but they kept an eye on Crosby just the same. Of course, I didn't tell them you guys were videoing him until they'd already seen him in action with their own eyes. Now there's no way Crosby can squirm out of this. The police have caught him with the goods."

"You sneaks!" Sue exclaimed. "Thanks for letting *me* in on the plan." Then her eyebrows knotted together in annoyance and she held up her camera. "And what about this video?"

"We'll take that," said a voice behind her.

Startled, Sue spun around and looked up into the face of one of the police officers. She hadn't seen him return.

"Oh," she said, dazedly handing him her camera.

The officer removed the cassette and handed the camera back.

"The more evidence, the better," he said. Then he smiled and headed back to the room where Crosby was.

Suddenly Sue had a thought. She whirled around.

"Will I get that back?" Sue called after the officer, and when Gina and Nicole started to giggle, she jammed her hands onto her hips and scowled at them. "What are you laughing at? Our CAGIS sleepover is on that cassette."

• • •

The three friends lurched down the aisle of the bus.

"*We* solved a crime!" Nicole bubbled, sliding into a seat. "That was so exciting!"

Gina shot her a disdainful glare. "Judging from the big lecture we got on leaving detective work to detectives, the police didn't seem all that impressed with our sleuthing," she said. "*Which*—I would like to point out—is exactly what I said all along."

"Okay," Sue conceded. "I admit it. You were right." Then her eyes

VIDEO CAMERA SURVEILLANCE

 While Sue was capturing the thief's actions on video, it is quite likely that his actions were also being seen by strategically placed surveillance cameras. After all, with so many valuable items in one place, the auction organizers would want to take all necessary precautions to protect them.

Surveillance cameras are becoming commonplace just about everywhere. Not only are they found in banks, museums, and retail stores, but they're popping up in other places as well. Office buildings, elevators, hotels, restaurants, sports venues, malls—anywhere large groups of people congregate or where items of value are found, there are probably surveillance cameras keeping an eye on things. Some people even have surveillance cameras in their homes. In fact, modern technology has made it possible to relay surveillance video via the Internet to anywhere on the planet.

Here's how it works. Suppose you want to make sure your brother doesn't snoop in your diary while you spend the weekend at a friend's house. You set up a surveillance camera in your room. He'll never notice it because modern cameras are so small and ordinary looking they're almost invisible. The camera is connected to a router that feeds the view of your room to the Internet. The Internet, in turn, forwards the video to you at your friend's house. To access it, all you have to do is enter a password. The process is completely private, or—if preferable—it can be made available to a network of computers.

Of course, if you can watch someone, who's to say someone isn't watching you too?

began to dance with mischief again. "But *you* have to admit that we weren't really ever in any danger, and it *was* our detective work that caught the crook. But next time, I promise we'll let the police solve the crime."

"Next time!" Gina exclaimed. "There isn't going to be a next time!" Then she turned toward the window, a clear indication that she didn't want to talk about the subject any more.

Sue and Nicole exchanged smirks and slid into the seat across the aisle. But they'd no sooner resumed their discussion than Gina jumped out of her seat, yanked on the cord, and dashed for the back door of the bus.

Startled, the two younger girls broke off their conversation and stared after her.

"What's the matter? What are you doing? Where are you going?" they demanded. And when the bus stopped and Gina pushed her way off without replying, they quickly jumped up too and raced after her.

But by the time their feet hit the sidewalk, Gina was already running back down the street in the direction from which they'd just come.

"Gina!" Nicole and Sue called, chasing after her.

Then Gina put on the brakes so abruptly they almost crashed into the back of her.

"What the—"

Gina just pointed.

"Look," she said. ★

ANIMATION EXPERIMENT

Because modern technology simplifies so many tasks, we often take it for granted. Consider Sue's video camera. Sixty years ago there were no such things as video cameras. Home movies became popular in the 1950s, but cameras were much more cumbersome, and viewing required developing the film, threading miles of it through a complicated machine, and projecting the images onto a screen or wall. The process certainly wasn't as simple as putting a disk into a camera, pressing a button, and then inserting the disk into a computer to view.

To appreciate how much technology has simplified the process of recording action, try the following experiment.

Materials:

* 20 pieces of blank paper cut into about 10-centimetre squares
* a coloured marker
* a shape pattern (such as a circle) that can be traced onto the paper

Procedure:

1. With the marker, trace the shape onto all the pieces of paper, making sure to move the shape into a slightly different position each time you trace it. For instance, if you want the circle to look like a bouncing ball, draw the first circle at the bottom of the first paper. On the next paper, draw it just a tiny bit higher. On the third paper, draw it a bit higher still. By the 10th paper, the circle should be at the top. Then use the next 10 papers to bring it down again. For a better effect, colour the shapes solidly.

2. When you've finished drawing, place the papers in a neat pile. *Be sure to keep the papers in order.*

3. Holding the pile tightly by one edge, use your other hand to flip the pages quickly from bottom to top so you can see the shape on each paper as it passes.

What Happened?

What did you notice about your shape? Did it move? The circle seemed to bounce when you flipped through the papers because of sensory memory. Sensory memory is like having a brief photographic memory of the image on our retina (see p. 18 for an explanation of the eye), which quickly fades away. Sensory memory lasts for a split second, so if you look at the first circle and look away, your mind still has a picture of the circle for a split second. If you look at the first page with the circle and flip to the next page at just the right speed, your sensory memory (that brief photographic memory) still holds the image of the first circle while you're seeing the second circle. The picture of the second circle will look as if it moved.

Electronically collected images seem to move because film and video play back thousands of individual pictures so quickly they seem like one continuous picture. All you have to do is put a video on pause to realize the action is actually a collection of many, many individual photographs—just like the bouncing ball you made.

More?

Now that you know how action photography works, can you make a more complicated action film—say one with a face that changes expression?

6

Out of Business

Nicole and Sue turned toward the small store Gina was pointing at and gasped.

It was on fire! The whole interior of the shop was engulfed in thick smoke and, near the back, angry orange flames were licking at the wall. Even standing on the sidewalk, Gina could feel the heat.

"We have to do something!" Nicole exclaimed.

But Gina was already ahead of her. She had the cellphone to her ear, and she was speaking urgently to someone on the other end.

"No, I can't tell if there's anyone inside," she said, frowning toward the building, "but I don't think so. The sign on the door says it's closed. Yes. Okay. We won't." Gina squinted at the name etched on the window in bold, gold lettering. "It's Barbara White Enterprises—553 Oak Street. Yes. I hear you. No, we won't. I promise."

Inside the building, the fire alarm was still ringing insistently, but almost the instant Gina broke the 911 connection, the wail of a distant siren could be heard above it.

"That was fast," Nicole said.

Gina shook her head. "The fire department was already on its way." Then she gestured toward the shop. "The place has a monitored fire alarm."

No sooner were the words out of her mouth than a woman came hurtling around the corner of the building, screaming, "No! No, no, no!" And before any of the girls could stop her, she was fumbling with a key in the door of the shop.

"You can't go in there!" Gina shouted to the woman. "It's boiling hot, and there could be an explosion any second! Wait for the fire department. Please!"

But the woman wasn't listening. She was consumed with her need to get into the building.

Gina looked around helplessly. There was no one else on the street, and from the sound of it, the fire truck was still a little bit away.

"C'mon!" she cried to her friends. "We can't let her go in there! Tackle her if you have to!"

The three girls charged the woman, but before they could reach her, she pushed open the door, causing a great plume of black smoke to pour through the opening like an evil genie escaping from a magic bottle. The force of the blast sent the woman reeling back-wards. She crashed into Gina, and then almost immediately began feeling her way back toward the store.

In seconds the street in front of the shop was fogged in by the deadly smoke. Gina's eyes stung and tears rolled down her cheeks. She pulled her shirt up over her nose and mouth, but the noxious fumes were everywhere, raking her throat and choking her. Half

THE DOPPLER EFFECT

 Have you ever noticed that a horn or a fire truck's siren seems to have a higher pitch when it is coming toward you and a lower pitch as it moves away from you? This is because the sound waves (see p. 25 for an explanation of sound waves) created by the horn are attached to a moving object (the car), and they get pushed together as the car approaches you, causing the waves to strike your ears with greater frequency. Remember that frequency is the number of sound waves per second. The horn always gives out the same frequency, but as the car approaches you, the same number of sound waves have to fit into less space and less time, so your ear hears a higher frequency. That makes the pitch of the horn seem higher.

As the car passes you and moves away, the same number of sound waves have to fit into more space and more time, which means there are fewer sound waves per second reaching your ear. Fewer sound waves per second reaching your ear means a lower-sounding frequency. As a result, the pitch of the horn seems lower. The horn hasn't changed; it just sounds like it has. This phenomenon is called the Doppler Effect, named after Christian Johann Doppler, who first identified it in 1842.

blind and coughing, she grabbed the other two girls, and together they stumbled away from the building.

Then the scream of the fire truck's siren became deafening, and suddenly there were firefighters and miles of grey hose everywhere.

A police car zoomed up to the curb, followed by an ambulance. Curious onlookers had started gathering too.

A firefighter appeared from nowhere and peered anxiously at the girls.

"Are you okay?" he asked.

The girls nodded, and Gina pointed toward the shop.

"But a lady went in there," she croaked.

"Inside the building?" His jaw tightened. "How long ago?"

"Just before you got here. We tried to stop her but—" Gina broke off, coughing.

The firefighter nodded grimly. "That's okay. Don't try to talk any more. I'll take care of it. You stay put." He pointed toward the paramedics getting out of the ambulance. "That man and woman will make sure you're all right." Then, without another word, he hurried back toward the burning building.

The ambulance attendants moved the girls farther away from the smoke and, after checking them over, pronounced them unhurt. What the girls needed most, they said, was lots of good fresh air.

The woman wasn't as lucky.

Less than a minute after rushing into the smoke, the firefighter stumbled back out with the woman slung over his shoulder. He took her directly to the paramedics. She was unconscious.

The girls watched in anxious silence as the paramedics swung into action. They worked quickly to make sure she was breathing. Then they checked her pulse and blood pressure, and flashed a light into her eyes. They put a mask over her nose and mouth—oxygen, Gina thought—and searched her body for any sign of burns. Eventually the woman came to, and—to Gina's amazement—almost immediately began struggling to get up and head back into the fire.

Gina couldn't believe it. She couldn't imagine what could possibly be so important to the woman that it was worth risking her life

CANCER AND FIREFIGHTING

Recent studies show there may be a link between firefighting and the development of some cancers—especially brain cancer and stomach cancer. So far, insurance providers and government committees concerned about their responsibilities to firefighters have done most of these studies.

Nevertheless, the increased number of firefighting cancer victims around the world has made the public more aware of the dangers of constant exposure to toxic, cancer-causing chemicals in smoke. Technically, smoke is carbon particles suspended in air and other gases. High amounts of any smoke are dangerous, but some smoke is worse than others. Just how bad a smoke is depends on its concentration (the number of carbon particles per unit of space—how thick the smoke is), which other gases are part of the smoke, how big the particles in the smoke are, and how long a person is exposed to the smoke. The dangerous chemicals in smoke mostly come from burning plastics and other artificial materials like paint, insulation, and glue. The burning of these materials produces the dangerous chemicals that coat the carbon particles and also produce harmful gases and vapours that get mixed in with the smoke. Firefighters wear protective equipment, but it isn't enough of a safeguard. Though more research needs to be done, U.S. and Ontario governments already acknowledge the connection and are willing to compensate firefighters who develop certain types of cancer.

for. Besides, whatever was inside that building, it had to have been destroyed by now. The woman was obviously not thinking straight.

But the paramedics were good at their job, managing to subdue her, and though she never stopped crying and moaning and gesturing toward the shop, they eventually got her into the ambulance.

The police took Gina, Sue, and Nicole home.

• • •

"Wow! Was that an exciting Saturday or what?" Sue proclaimed as Gina opened the door to her the next day.

"Sshhh," Gina hissed. "Not so loud. My mother was up practically all night wringing her hands. One minute she was sure that Crosby was going to come looking for revenge, and the next minute she was worrying that my lungs had been permanently damaged by all that smoke. It took me almost two hours to convince her that I'd already been checked out by the paramedics and didn't need to go to the hospital." She peered down the hall. "So keep your voice down. I don't want to get her started again."

Then she led Sue downstairs to the rec room. Nicole was already there, poring over the Sunday paper, searching for articles about the fire and the auction thefts.

"Here it is," she announced, waving a section of the paper in the air. When she had the other girls' attention, she began to read. "A local man was arrested yesterday in connection with a rash of pickpocket thefts that have plagued the city for the last several months. The suspect, a reputable seeing-eye dog trainer, was apprehended at an antique auction yesterday where, while posing as a blind person, he is thought to have relieved at least six people of their wallets. The man is in custody and will be arraigned in court tomorrow. His dog is in the care of the authorities."

"It didn't say anything about us," Sue pouted.

"That's just as well," Gina said. "Otherwise my mother would probably enrol me in a witness protection program and ship me off to Siberia or some other glamorous place. Besides, I'm sure the police don't want to give away all their information—just in case."

"Just in case...*what*?" Sue asked.

Gina shrugged. "I don't know. But I'm sure it's policy or something, not to disclose too many details."

"Do you think we'll have to testify in court?" Nicole asked. "I'd be too nervous to get up on the stand."

Gina shook her head. "I doubt it. The police have so much evidence they won't need our testimony. The guy will probably just confess."

"Here's the story about the fire," Nicole announced, pointing to the paper. "It was buried on page three of the local news section."

"What does it say?" Sue asked. "Does it mention us?"

"Sort of, but not really," Nicole replied.

"Read it," Sue said.

Nicole cleared her throat.

"Firefighters were called to a blaze at Barbara White Enterprises, 553 Oak Street, late yesterday morning. Damage is estimated at $600,000. There were no serious injuries, though three girls at the scene received treatment for minor smoke inhalation, and Barbara White, a well-known inventor and proprietor of the office, was taken to hospital for observation. She was later released. Arson is suspected."

"Arson!" Sue exclaimed. "They think somebody started that fire on purpose?"

"Well, if somebody did, it sure wasn't Barbara White," Gina said. "If she'd sabotaged her own office, I'm sure she would have taken her valuables out of it first."

"What do you mean?" Nicole asked.

"I mean, that lady was trying so hard to get into the burning building, there had to be something inside that she really wanted."

"No kidding," Nicole agreed.

"Hmmph," Gina mused aloud. "I wonder what it was." ✦

ROLLOVERS, FLASHOVERS, AND BACKDRAFTS

Used properly, fire is one of the most valuable tools people possess, but out of control, it is a monster to be feared.

Many people assume that those unlucky enough to be trapped in a fire die of their burns. The truth is that asphyxiation (suffocation) is the main killer, attacking its victims in a number of ways. A raging fire consumes all the available oxygen, producing poisonous smoke filled with carbon monoxide and other toxic gases. Breathing it in for even a short period of time can be fatal. In addition to its toxicity, the smoke can also be unbearably hot, sizzling the lungs of anyone who inhales it.

Smoke presents other dangers as well. Because it is hot, it rises and accumulates at the highest point in a room or building. If the gases in it aren't allowed to escape, they will eventually explode. This explosion can take two forms.

The first is called a rollover. Reaching temperatures greater than 400° C, the smoke ignites the fuel around it (such as a ceiling) and races across it, much as an ocean wave crashes onto shore.

PRESSURE EXPERIMENT
Part 1

Fire needs three things. First, it must have *fuel*. Fuel is any combustible substance (something that can burn). The second requirement is a *temperature* high enough to cause combustion. And finally, it must have *oxygen*. If any of these factors cease to be present, the fire will die.

Though a rollover is terrifying and deadly, a flashover is worse. It is also caused by the overheating of trapped gases in smoke, but instead of starting in one place and racing across a space, a flashover ignites everything in one instant. Those caught in a flashover do not survive.

To avoid rollovers and flashovers, firefighters immediately vent fire sites to eliminate the heat and pressure of smoke buildup. They do this by opening windows or chopping through roofs or walls. However, venting can cause problems too. If a burning building is vented in the wrong place, a backdraft can occur. The fire, looking for a fresh supply of fuel, takes in a huge amount of air through the new vent and then releases it again in one mighty blast, much like a fire-breathing dragon. Even trained firefighters have little or no defence against rollovers, flashovers, and backdrafts.

During a blaze in a contained space such as a building, pressure created by the fire builds up. But because the air outside the structure is pushing back with equal force, equilibrium (balance) is maintained. However, if the fire becomes so great that it creates more pressure inside the structure than outside, the structure will explode. That is why firefighters ventilate burning buildings. They want to equalize the pressure.

Here's an experiment to illustrate how equilibrium works.

Materials:
* a plastic pop or water bottle (1 litre or larger)
* a balloon

Procedure:
1. Blow up the balloon and observe what happens. If you think of the air you are blowing into the balloon as pressure, and the air outside the balloon as pressure also, which of the two pressures is greater? What do you think would happen if you continued to blow into the balloon?
2. Now try to blow into the bottle and observe what happens. Does the bottle expand as the balloon did? What would happen if you could blow hard enough to create more pressure inside the bottle than around the outside of it?
3. Now let the air out of the balloon and push the non-blowing end of the balloon into the bottle. Then, stretch the opening of the balloon over the opening of the bottle so the balloon is secured tightly around the mouth of the bottle while dangling inside it. Try to blow up the balloon and observe what happens.

What Happened?

When the balloon was inside the bottle, you couldn't blow it up, no matter how hard you tried. You couldn't blow up the balloon when it was inside the bottle because there was something else in there taking up space: air! The air was trapped inside the bottle by the balloon stretched over the opening, and the air in the bottle was exerting force on the air inside the balloon when you tried to blow it up.

Air normally exerts force on a balloon when we blow it up, but the air inside the bottle had two forces acting on it: the force of the air inside the balloon when you were trying to blow it up, and the force of the walls of the bottle. Think of the forces within the bottle as being the same as if you were pushing on a wall; you are exerting pressure on the wall and the wall is exerting pressure on you. This is Newton's Third Law of motion: every action has an equal and opposite reaction.

PRESSURE EXPERIMENT

Part 2

There is one way to blow up the balloon inside the bottle. Have this experiment ready to go the next time you try Part 1 of this experiment with a friend. You can fool your friends into thinking you have the lungs of a super hero!

Materials:
* a glass bottle
* a balloon
* a water tap

Procedure:

1. Take your bottle and stick the round end of the balloon into it, but leave a little bit of the neck sticking out of the bottle.

2. Turn on the tap so that very warm (but not hot) water is running, and, holding the bottle on its side by the neck, stick the body of the bottle under the warm water. You should hold the bottle under the warm water for at least five minutes. The longer you leave the bottle under the warm water, the better the experiment will work.

3. After five minutes, put the bottle down on the counter so that it is sitting upright. Quickly stretch the mouth of the balloon over the neck of the bottle like you did in Part 1 of the experiment. It's important that you do this step very quickly before the bottle starts to cool down.

4. Put the bottle in the freezer and leave it there for 10 minutes.

5. After 10 minutes, take your bottle out of the freezer and look at the balloon!

What Happened?

The balloon blew up inside the bottle! Why? Read the facing page on matter to help you understand this explanation. We started by heating up the bottle with warm water. But the main purpose of the warm water wasn't to heat up the bottle but to heat up the air inside the bottle. Once the air inside the bottle heated up, it expanded. That meant some of the air had to move out of the bottle because the warm air took up more space than when it was cooler. Since some of the air moved out of the bottle when it was heated up, there were fewer air molecules in the bottle. When you took the bottle out from under the warm water, you covered the bottle opening with the balloon. This trapped the air inside and prevented more air from moving in or out of the bottle. When you put the bottle in the freezer,

MATTER

Matter is the stuff everything is made of. The air you breathe, the juice you drink, your bicycle, even *you* are made up of matter. Matter is made up of molecules. Molecules are very small (too small for us to see), and different molecules make up different things (a water molecule looks different from a sugar molecule). Molecules never touch one another, and there is a lot of empty space in between each molecule. There are three states of matter: solid, liquid, and gas. The molecules in the solid state are quite rigid and don't move around; they just vibrate in their place. The molecules in the liquid state are a bit farther apart from each other than those in the solid state and move around a lot more, but they are still limited. The molecules in the gas state have the most space between them and move everywhere and anywhere they can.

When an object is heated up, it expands, and when it cools down, it contracts (gets smaller). The molecules themselves don't change size when this happens; the space between the molecules changes in size. So, when something is cooled down, the molecules come closer to each other, just the way you and your friends huddle together to stay warm on a cold winter day. When something is heated up, the molecules spread apart from each other, just like when it's really hot outside and you don't want to be near anyone else. This expanding and contracting with cold and heat happens the most with gases because the molecules are the freest in gases, and they can easily spread apart and move closer together. Solids expand and shrink the least with heat and cold because their molecules have a much harder time moving around. They can only spread apart and move closer together a little bit.

the air started to cool down and take up less space. But more air couldn't rush into the bottle to equalize the pressure because the balloon had sealed off the opening of the bottle. Air could move into the balloon, though, which was in the bottle. The balloon expanded and took up the space left by the cooler air.

More?

We've all sat around a campfire or in front of a fireplace on a cold night. Paper and kindling are used to start the fire because the temperature at which they will ignite is quite low. If you hold a match up to a log, the log doesn't burst into flame the way the paper does. The temperature of the fire must get hotter before the log will burn. When we want the fire to die, we stop adding wood. In other words, we take away the fuel, because that is easier than lowering the temperature or taking away the oxygen. But if the fire was small enough, you could.

Here's something to try with an adult. Place a tea light or votive candle (fuel) in a safe holder and light it (temperature). After it has burned for a minute or two, place a large empty jar over the candle and observe what happens. Think in terms of what fire needs to exist.

Fire needs oxygen to exist. When the jar is placed over the candle, the amount of oxygen available to the fire is limited to the amount in the jar. When the oxygen in the jar is consumed, the fire goes out because it no longer has the oxygen it needs to exist.

7

Something Uncanny

Later that afternoon, the Science Squad was once again at 553 Oak Street.

"Well, here we are—back at the scene of the crime," Nicole announced, spreading her arms to take in what was left of the building that had once housed Barbara White Enterprises. "Though I haven't got the faintest idea *why*," she added under her breath.

Gina stared wide-eyed at the burned-out concrete shell. "Gosh," she murmured. "It sure looks different."

The front door was boarded over. So was the plate-glass window, and above it, where the day before there had been an awning, all that was left was a charred metal frame. On the walls, soot wisped skyward from the tops of the window and door like charcoal feathers. But lower, where the spray from fire hoses had splattered the smoke against the whitewashed exterior, the wall was simply grimy black. On the sidewalk, water lingered in oily rainbow puddles.

Gina noticed an unhappy face someone had drawn in the soot. *How appropriate*, she thought.

Nicole frowned and shook her head. "Can you imagine losing everything in a fire? That would be awful."

Sue and Gina nodded.

"But it could have been worse," Gina pointed out. "That lady could have lost her life in there. In fact, she almost did. If it hadn't been for the firefighters and paramedics, she probably would have."

"She should thank her lucky stars she wasn't living 150 years ago," Sue said. "Back then she wouldn't have had any chance at all."

"Why do you say that?" Nicole asked.

"Mainly because everything was a lot slower," Sue told her. "For one thing, people were the ones who sounded the alarm—not smoke and fire detectors. And fire engines weren't motorized like they are now. Back in those days, they were pulled by horses—or humans. There weren't fire hydrants to hook the hoses up to either. The water had to be hand-pumped from a big vat on the fire truck, and that had to be constantly refilled using buckets, so if there was no water supply nearby, the firefighters didn't stand a chance."

The girls took another long look at the destruction caused by the previous day's blaze. Despite what Sue had said, Gina found it hard to imagine things could have been worse.

"So why did you want to come here, Gina? You're not usually the one who wants to chase down a mystery. What do you think we're going to find?" Nicole asked.

Gina pushed her hair back from her face and pursed her mouth in thought. What *was* she hoping to discover? "I'm not really sure," she replied. "I guess I'm hoping we'll discover what the woman wanted inside that building. It just doesn't make sense to me. I could understand if she'd been trying to rescue someone, but what *thing* could possibly be worth risking her life for?"

Sue leaned close and whispered, "If you really want to know, why don't you ask her?" Then she nodded at a woman coming down the sidewalk toward them. "There she is now."

Barbara White saw the Science Squad at the same instant Gina saw her. Immediately the woman stopped, and the expression of worry on her face changed to a scowl. Then, just as quickly, she was on the move again, but this time at a run.

"Are you trying to steal from me too?" she demanded, pushing at the girls. "Get away from my office!"

Surprised, the girls backed off.

"It's okay," Gina said, raising her hands defensively and trying to calm the woman at the same time. "We weren't doing anything—honest. We were just looking. Don't you recognize us?" When Barbara White's scowl deepened, Gina added, "We were here yesterday during the fire. We're the ones who tried to keep you from going inside. Don't you remember?"

The woman's eyes narrowed skeptically as she studied the girls more closely. And then without warning, Barbara White completely broke down and began crying in loud uncontrolled sobs.

Gina automatically put an arm around the distraught woman to comfort her.

"Don't cry," she soothed her. "Don't cry. I know it looks bad right now, but it'll be okay. You'll see. Your insurance company will pay for the repairs, and before you know it, your office will be as good as new."

Barbara White shook her head and began to wail louder than ever.

"No, no, no! You don't understand. It's too late. It was on the computer! Everything—my design, the scale drawings, the production figures, my proposal. Everything I needed to file for the patent was in there!" She gestured toward the burned building and then buried her face in her hands. "This was my last chance. This invention was all I had left! Now what am I going to do? I'm ruined!"

Nicole and Sue exchanged uneasy glances.

"You still have the idea," Nicole suggested cautiously. "I know it would take some time, but couldn't you draw your invention again?"

"You don't understand," the woman sobbed. "There's no time. I was only a day or two ahead of Charles. I was almost ready to file my patent application. There were only a couple of minor adjustments …but now…" she broke off.

"Who is Charles?" Sue asked innocently, but from the way Barbara White reacted, she might as well have been baiting a ferocious lion.

The woman lashed out angrily. "Who *is* he?" she demanded, her eyes flashing. "He is the one who stole my idea for the entropy relocator. He is the one who started this fire!"

"Those are pretty serious accusations," Nicole said. "Do you have any proof?"

"Nothing the police will believe. But the fact that he walked out on me and our marriage just when I was getting close to filing for the patent is proof enough for me. Besides, if he didn't start this fire, then who did?"   •

"Charles is your husband?" Sue asked. "Why would your husband want to destroy your business and steal your invention?"

"So he could have it for himself," Barbara White growled back. "This is a revolutionary development. It means we will be able to recapture lost energy, and change it back into a usable form. Our world would have a safe and continuous supply of energy forever! Do you know what an invention like this will mean to the environment? Do you have any idea how much money it's going to be worth? It would make me a billionaire many times over! You just wait. In a few days Charles will file for the patent, and there'll be nothing I can do about it." Then she broke into tears once more.

Gina patted her on the back. "Now, now. Don't start crying again. That's not going to help. Why don't we take a look around here? The fire department has the place boarded up, so we won't be able to go inside—it would be too dangerous anyway—but maybe we can find some clues outside."

The woman took the tissue Gina offered her and allowed herself to be led around to the side of the building. Everybody studied the ground intently, but aside from some sodden cardboard coffee cups and soggy cigarette butts, there was nothing much to see.

"What's around the back?" Nicole asked.

"A back entrance to the office, a couple of parking spaces, and the garbage bin," Barbara White sniffed. "That's about it."

"Garbage bin?" Sue perked up. "That could be good for some clues. Let's check it out," she said, running on ahead.

"Hey," she called back as she neared the rear of the building, "there's a car here."

Immediately, the others picked up speed. The sidewalk was still wet after the fire, and their footsteps slapped noisily on the pavement, so that when they thundered around the corner of Barbara White Enterprises, they startled a man balanced precariously over the large, blue trash container, and he fell partway in.

For a few seconds, all anyone could see were black shoes and grey pants waving madly in the air. But finally the fellow found his balance again and pushed himself out and back onto solid ground. In an instant, he whirled around, yelling.

"What in blue blazes are you trying to prove, scaring me like…"

But as he saw who he was speaking to, his voice trailed off.

And then Barbara White took a step back and gasped.

"Charles!" ★

89

THERMODYNAMICS

Over the years, scientists have identified pollutants in our air. To tackle this pollution problem, engineers have developed equipment, called emission control devices, to reduce pollution. Laws now require that cars and many industries use these devices. The same sorts of measures have been adopted with regard to the world's water supply, so that our waterways can remain safe habitats for animals and plants. Forests are no longer cut down indiscriminately. Endangered animals are protected.

Everywhere, people are becoming more and more environmentally aware, and the watchwords are reduce, reuse, recycle. Where once people took the resources of the earth for granted, they are now taking steps to safeguard them for the future. Scientists, technologists, and engineers are playing important roles in protecting our environment.

One important area of research is the search for alternative energy supplies. In the past, energy was provided largely by non-renewable fossil fuels such as wood, coal, oil, and natural gas. But every day, innovative renewable alternatives are being discovered and developed. Hydroelectricity, wind power, and solar energy have been around for quite a while, but geothermal energy and tidal power are still pretty new.

One energy alternative that is becoming popular is the recycling of waste, an excellent idea considering the average North American throws away more than 700 kilograms of garbage a year! Scientists have discovered that rotting garbage produces a gas called methane. This colourless, odourless gas has very similar properties to natural gas. Consequently, it can be used as fuel but is very explosive. That is why government rules in the United States and other places require landfills to collect this gas. It is then purified and converted to a liquid called methanol, which can be piped into natural gas pipelines. Methane gas is a greenhouse gas related to global warming. So collecting methane and using it for fuel instead of allowing it to escape into the atmosphere is reducing greenhouse gas emissions, which is good for the environment too. This process of reclaiming methane gas is becoming popular all over the world, though it probably works best in the city of Florence, Alabama, where 1 million cubic metres of methane gas are recovered every day! Even in India, where cows are sacred, cow manure is converted to methane to produce electricity.

In our story, Barbara White invented a new, environmentally friendly energy source. Her invention used the first and second laws of thermodynamics. The first law of thermodynamics states that energy cannot be created or destroyed, only changed from one form to another. The second law of thermodynamics says that when energy changes from one form to another, it always changes into a more disorganized form, which eventually becomes unavailable for use (scientists call this unusable energy entropy). In any change of energy, some energy is lost to entropy. Barbara White thought up a way to defy the second law of thermodynamics and to recapture lost energy without using any extra energy to find it. This means that the energy would always be renewable so we wouldn't have to burn any fuels like coal or gas or be left with nuclear waste from nuclear reactors.

ENERGY EXPERIMENT

Wind and water are excellent energy resources because they are available on a large scale, and they are renewable.

Long ago, mills ground grain into flour using water power. Early sailors relied on the wind to push their ships. Paddlewheel boats used steam. Harnessed on a larger scale, wind and water can power entire communities.

Here is an experiment to illustrate how wind can provide us with power.

Materials:
* a 10-centimetre square of heavy paper
* a straight pin
* scissors
* a straw
* hair dryer (optional)

Procedure:
1. Lining up opposite corners, fold the paper in half to form a triangle.
2. Then fold the triangle in half again to form a smaller triangle.
3. Unfold the paper and cut about six centimetres along each fold line. Be careful not to cut all the way to the centre of the paper.
4. Working in a clockwise direction, take the corner of each triangle and place it on the centre of the square.
5. When you have done this for all four triangles, poke the straight pin through all layers to hold them in place.
6. Then poke the pin through the end of a straw so the straw acts like a handle; bend the end of the pin downward so that the pin doesn't poke you or come out of the straw.

7. You've created a windmill. Blow on it from various angles. Turn the hair dryer on and place the windmill up to that. If it is a breezy day, hold the windmill to the wind. Hold it up in the air and run with it.

What Happened?

When did the blades of your windmill move? When didn't they move? What direction did they move in? When did they move the fastest? What conclusions can you draw about wind as an energy source? When you blow on your windmill, your diaphragm (a muscle below the lungs) contracts, pushing the air in your lungs through your windpipe and out your mouth. The air pushed out of your lungs exerts a force on the blades of the windmill, causing it to move. The harder you blow, the more force you exert on the windmill, and the faster it will move. The energy from the moving windmill can be converted into other kinds of energy.

More?

Wind, when harnessed to a generator, can be a powerful energy source. However, conditions are not always windy. Fortunately, the same windy effect can be artificially created. Here is something else for you to try. *But make sure you have an adult helping you with this one!*

Place water in a pot, cover the pot with a lid, and place over heat. When the water is boiling so that steam is escaping from the pot in a forceful stream, hold your windmill up to the stream. But be sure to keep your hand away from the steam! What happened to the blades of your windmill?

PATENTS

People who ask the question "What if...?" often become writers or inventors. Writers turn *what ifs* into stories; inventors turn them into technological innovations. Inventions can be as simple as redesigning the grip on a paintbrush, or they may be as intricate as the creation of an artificial heart.

Because necessity is the mother of invention, all of us have invented things to meet an immediate need—a piece of cardboard may act as a dustpan, a credit card becomes an ice scraper, a plastic bag is used as a raincoat. These are indeed inventions, but they aren't things we would want to use all the time. However, inventions that have the potential to revolutionize the way people live also have the potential to make their inventors a lot of money, and because of that, inventors seek licences called patents, which keep other people from making, selling, or using their inventions without permission for 20 years. That's how long a patent is in effect, though it can be renewed.

Patent offices are government-operated, and rules for patents may change from country to country. Generally, only inventions may be patented; methods for doing things may not, so that a cooking utensil may be given a patent but not the ways to use it. If more than one person applies for the same patent, it is usually the first person to apply who gets it.

But obtaining a patent is a slow process. It is also complicated and expensive. This is how it works in Canada.

To begin, a search is done to see if someone else has already been granted a patent for that particular invention. For this step, the inventor must provide photographs, drawings, and descriptions of the invention, explaining how it is made and used, how it can be modified, and what its advantages are. This first phase can cost from $500 to $1500 and doesn't guarantee that a patent will be granted.

If the search shows there is no existing patent, the inventor resubmits this information along with a statement indicating the type of patent protection wanted. The usual cost of submitting this application is about $4000, but it can be more for complicated inventions.

Now it is time for the patent office to "prosecute" the application. This means thoroughly testing out the invention, a process that can cost another $800 to $5000 and may take two or more years.

Then, if the patent is finally granted, the inventor must pay a yearly maintenance fee of $150 to $600 (on average) to keep the patent active.

This might sound discouraging to prospective inventors, but if an invention is really good, industries that would benefit from the invention are often willing to pay for the patent application in exchange for the right to produce and market the invention when the patent is finally granted.

8

What's in a Name?

For several very long seconds, the man and woman stared at each other while the Science Squad looked on. It was Charles who broke the silence.

Something about the way he tensed and took a half step back reminded Gina of a frightened animal preparing to bolt. Eyeing Barbara White warily, he asked, "Who are you?"

That was an odd question for a man to ask his wife, Gina thought, frowning.

"Don't start that again, Charles," Barbara White warned him.

The man looked relieved. "So you *are* Barbara," he said.

The woman clucked her tongue in disgust. "Of course, I'm Barbara. That's not the point." Then her eyes narrowed and she jammed her hands onto her hips. "The real question is—what are you doing here—" she gestured toward the trash bin and added, "picking through my garbage? Are you trying to steal more secrets?"

Charles rolled his eyes and sighed wearily. "I haven't stolen any secrets."

"Oh, really," Barbara sneered. "Then why did you set that fire yesterday and what did you take out of the garbage?"

All eyes immediately shifted to what Charles was holding in his hand. He looked down too.

"It's certainly no secret," he said, holding up a wrapper from a candy bar. "But I think it proves who started the fire."

"Gulp!" Nicole squeaked, and everyone turned to look at her. "It wasn't me—honest!" she grimaced, pulling an identical wrapper from her jacket pocket. It contained a partially eaten bar of chocolate. She shrugged sheepishly. "I just happen to like the same candy bar. I sure didn't start any fire though." She glanced around at all the eyes upon her. Then she broke off a piece of chocolate and said, "Anybody want some?"

"Don't mind if I do," Barbara White said, snatching the square of chocolate from Nicole and popping it into her mouth.

"NO!" Charles bellowed, charging across the pavement and grabbing Barbara White roughly by the arm.

She pulled away and glared at him.

"What in the world is wrong with you? It's not enough that you destroy my chance for success with the entropy relocator—now you're trying to steal food right out of my mouth!"

"Be reasonable, Barbara," he pleaded. "You know what the doctor said."

To everyone's surprise, Barbara White threw her head back and laughed. Then she leaned forward and gave Charles a kiss on the cheek. "That old fuddy-duddy? He just doesn't want us to have any fun. But you do, don't you, Charlie?" She winked.

Gina blinked and her mouth dropped open. She'd never seen anyone change moods that fast in her life.

Charles must have felt the same way because his eyes opened wide as he whispered, "Barbara?"

Barbara White laughed again. Then she removed the elastic holding her hair in a tight ponytail, freeing it to cascade over her shoulders. "No, silly. It's Barbie."

Charles closed his eyes and shook his head. "I knew it," he mumbled. "It was you. You're the one who started the fire, aren't you?"

"Now don't go getting all serious on me," she pouted. "Barbara does enough of that for all of us. She really needs to lighten up." Barbie looked down at her clothes and shook her head. "And she could start by getting some new clothes. The woman dresses like she's eighty years old. No wonder you left her."

"I didn't leave," Charles protested, but Barbie waved away his objection.

"You don't have to explain to me," she said. "I understand perfectly. Barbara is such a whiner, no one could live with her. You know what her problem is, don't you?" But before Charles could answer, she continued, "She has no idea how to have fun." Her eyes glittered mischievously. "But I do."

Fishing keys out of her handbag, she ran to the driver's side of the parked car, climbed in, and started the engine, revving it so hard the noise was deafening, and Gina was sure the car was either going to explode or become airborne. Then the window on the passenger's side slid down and Barbie called, "Hop in, Charlie, and we'll take a little spin."

Charles looked uncertain. "Maybe I better drive," he called back.

Barbie shook her head. "I'm going to have some fun. Come with me—or don't. It's up to you." She paused briefly and then took her foot off the accelerator and slipped the car into gear. "It's your last chance."

Charles hesitated for just a fraction of a second before opening the passenger door and throwing himself into the seat beside her. Then with a great rumble from the engine and a screeching of tires, the car tore off down the street.

The members of the Science Squad stared dumbly at one another. Throughout the entire exchange between Barbara White and her husband, the girls had stood in stunned silence, mesmerized by what was happening. It was as if they'd been watching a play and had hardly dared breath too loud for fear of missing part of the action.

But now that the actors had left the stage, the spell was broken.

"Oooo-eeee!" Sue exclaimed. "That was like watching *The Incredible Hulk*. I'm surprised the woman didn't turn green and burst through her clothes."

"No kidding," Nicole nodded. "What *was* that? I've never seen anything like it. Talk about Dr. Jekyll and Mr. Hyde. Except instead of drinking a chemical potion, Barbara White lost it by eating a measly little piece of chocolate." She took the remainder of her chocolate bar and tossed it into the trash bin. "Was it poison?"

"Sort of," Gina said with an air of authority that made the other girls turn to look at her. "But only to Barbara."

"You mean I chucked out my candy bar for nothing!" Nicole complained, looking longingly at the trash bin. Then she eyed Gina suspiciously. "Okay, Einstein," she said, "what do you know that we don't?"

Gina shrugged. "Maybe nothing—but if you ask me, we just had a glimpse of a classic case of Dissociative Identity Disorder."

"What's that?" Nicole asked.

Gina grinned. "It used to be called Multiple Personality Disorder, but since doctors have learned more about the condition, they feel that Dissociative Identity is a more accurate way to describe it.

We all have multiple parts to our personalities, but most of us are able to blend them into one person. D.I.D. people can't do that. So for them, it's like having a bunch of different people living inside one body."

"So Barbara and Barbie are two different people?" Sue said.

ALBERT EINSTEIN

When people consider the brain's vast abilities, many of them think of Albert Einstein – and for good reason. Though Einstein died almost 50 years ago, his contributions to science live on. He won the Nobel Prize in 1921 for his 1905 work with light. He identified the connection between energy and mass (Theory of Relativity), which he expressed in the equation $E = mc^2$.

By most people's standards, Einstein was a genius. *Time* magazine even went so far as to name him the Person of the Century! The scientific community was so impressed with his mind that after he died in 1955, his brain was removed, preserved, and studied to see what made his thought processes superior to those of other people. At first, researchers found no major differences, but in 1996 much of Einstein's brain came into the hands of Dr. Sandra Witelson, who studies brain structure and function at McMaster University in Hamilton, Ontario, Canada.

By comparing Einstein's brain with others, Witelson discovered that one section responsible for mathematical thought seemed about 15 percent denser than normal. As well, a groove

Gina made a face. "Not really." She scratched her head, searching for a way to explain. Then, coming up with an idea, her expression cleared again and she continued. "Think of it this way. Sue, you know how when you get excited you…" she hesitated, "shall we say—start to bounce?"

called the Sylvan fissure, which slices through the brain, seemed quite a bit smaller, causing Einstein's brain cells (neurons) to be closer together than is usual. Some scientists believe this allowed for more neural connections, which in turn, could have made Einstein a more insightful thinker.

That's very interesting, especially considering that when Einstein was a child, his parents worried he might have learning disabilities. He didn't speak until he was three years old, and he did poorly at school. In fact, he dropped out when he was just 15. Some people speculate that Einstein might have suffered from Attention Deficit Disorder (ADD), but since he was never tested for the condition, there is no way to know for sure. Others believe he just didn't fit into the educational mould. He needed more freedom than the German school system allowed. At any rate, his teachers considered him a negative influence on the other students and were glad to see him leave.

Imagine their surprise when he went on to become not only a world-renowned physicist but a respected humanitarian as well.

Sue's eyes narrowed. "What's wrong with that? It's very expressive."

Gina wagged her hand impatiently and pushed on with her explanation. "But when you get all caught up in a daydream, you suddenly get very still and quiet."

Sue jammed her hands onto her hips. "What is this—pick on Sue day?"

"It's true, Sue," Nicole interjected. "You do get really quiet when you're thinking about something. That's not a *bad* thing," she added quickly.

"Of course, it's not," Gina agreed. "The point is that both those things are part of your personality. But they're blended together. If you had D.I.D. though, the part of you that bounces would probably never daydream, and the quiet part of you would never get excited. You would be one personality or the other, but not both together, because those parts of your personality would be dissociated."

"Oh, I get it," Sue said, her body relaxing once more. "That's weird. Is that what you think is going on with Barbara White?"

Gina nodded.

"Wow!" Sue murmured. And then, "Do her different identities know about each other?"

"Maybe," Gina shrugged. "Barbie seems to know about Barbara, but I'm not sure Barbara knows about Barbie—or the others."

"Others?" Nicole said. "There are others?"

"Probably. People who suffer from D.I.D. usually have several dissociated personalities—at least three, and sometimes even ten or more."

"Man, that would be like having two basketball teams in your own body!" Sue said.

"What causes D.I.D.?" Nicole asked.

"Well, according to the D.I.D. documentary I watched, it is almost always caused by abuse. Children who are abused are the

NEURONS

 Cells in the nervous system are called neurons. The brain has about 100 billion of them, and each one is connected to about 1000 others. Neurons gather and store sensory information and transmit messages to other parts of the body.

There are many different types of neurons, but they all contain the same three basic parts: a cell body, dendrites, and an axon. The cell body changes nutrients to energy and acts as the drop-off and pickup location for the dendrites and axon. The dendrites carry sensory information to the cell body, and the axon carries information away from the cell body to other parts of the body. To get an idea of what a neuron is like, all you have to do is look at your hand. The fleshy part that contains your palm is like the cell body of the neuron. Your fingers represent dendrites, and your arm is like the axon.

main victims. Dissociating the different parts of their personalities is their way of coping with what's happened to them."

"Is there a cure?"

"Well, there aren't pills you can take or an operation," Gina told them, "but psychotherapy helps people face the cause of their disorder and teaches them to live with it. Some people become quite good at blending their dissociated parts back together. And some D.I.D. people don't even try. Once they understand what's going on, they're happy living with all their different identities."

"And so you think that Barbara Wh—"

Sue's question was cut short by the return of the car that Barbara White and her husband had left in just moments before. But now Charles was driving, and he was alone. The car screeched to a halt beside the Science Squad. Then the door flew open, and Charles jumped out and strode toward them.

"I want to talk to you girls," he said.

BRAIN PROTECTION EXPERIMENT

The brain controls the human nervous system. Everything we do—speak, run, laugh, breathe, cry—is controlled by our brains. And that's fine – unless the brain isn't functioning properly.

There are all sorts of things that can cause the brain to malfunction—genetics, trauma, aging, stroke, depression, drug addiction, illness—to name a few. Most brain disorders are unforeseeable and unavoidable, but there is one that we can take steps to prevent, and that is head/brain injury.

The brain is very powerful, but it is also very fragile. It is surrounded by fluid and protected by the bones of the skull, but it is far from indestructible. So whenever people are taking part in activities that could result in a blow to the head, they should wear a protective helmet. Hockey players, mountain climbers, boxers, inline skaters, construction workers, cyclists, race drivers, and river rafters should all wear helmets.

Let's try an experiment to see why.

Materials:

* ✳ two uncooked eggs in their shells
* ✳ felt-tipped marker
* ✳ newspaper
* ✳ whatever you can think of to make a helmet

Procedure:

1. In this experiment, the eggs represent the human brain. (The yolk is the brain and the shell is the skull.) Imagine your eggs are mountain climbers. Use the marker to draw faces on the eggs so they look like heads.

2. For this next part, work outside, in the basement, or in a garage. Spread newspaper to protect the floor. Stand over the paper and drop (don't throw) one of the eggs. What happened?

3. To protect the remaining egg, design and construct a safety helmet for it. Make sure your helmet encircles the entire egg, since you don't know which side of the egg will hit the ground. What sorts of materials would make good protectors? Why? What features should your helmet possess? *Remember:* Your helmet should be reasonably sized. After all, mountain climbers need to protect their heads, but that protection mustn't interfere with their climb.

4. When your helmet is complete, put it on your egg and test it by dropping the egg on the newspaper as you did before.

With friends, see who can design the most effective and efficient helmet.

What Happened?

Did your helmet protect the egg? If not, why not? What improvements could you make? The purpose of a helmet is to diffuse (spread out) the energy of something hitting it. A cushioning device is used to absorb the energy and reduce the speed of the egg (or your head) so that it won't be damaged. The cushioning device acts like a spring to slow down the speed at which the egg hits the ground. So rather than the egg hitting a hard surface and coming to an abrupt stop, the cushioning device would act like a spring and allow the egg to slow down while the spring compresses. Our knees do the same thing. When we land after doing a jump, we bend our knees. Our knees act like a compressing spring to slow down the speed at which we land.

More?
Head injuries can be caused even without receiving a blow to the head. A severe shake can cause brain injury. Take an egg and give it a good shake. Then crack it into a bowl. Is the yolk unbroken?

$\sqrt{225}$

NaCl

H_2O

$A^2 + B^2 = C^2$

CO_2

0010
1010
0100
1100
1011
1000
0101
1110
0110
0001

9

Who's Who?

Unconsciously, the girls moved closer together, and Gina, being the oldest—even though she was just as apprehensive as her friends—took a small step forward to meet Charles White.

"What do you want?" She cringed at the sound of her own voice when the cool, calm, and collected tone she'd been striving for came out as a snarl. She cleared her throat and tried again. "What I mean is, why do you want to talk to us?"

Charles White stuffed his hands into his pants' pocket. His frown deepened. "I don't really know how to put this," he confessed with a shrug. "It's just that you seem to know my wife, Barbara, but when I asked Barbie who you were, she had no idea, and so I…" his voice trailed off. He heaved a frustrated sigh and raked his hands through his hair. "It's very confusing. You see, my wife suffers from –"

"Dissociative Identity Disorder?" Sue peeked out from behind Gina.

Charles dropped his hands and the frown on his face turned to confusion. "Why... yes, but...how did you know? Did Barbara tell you?"

Nicole peeked out around the other side of Gina and shook her head. "She didn't have to," she told him. "She has all the classic symptoms."

Gina looked at her friends and rolled her eyes. A little information had turned them into a couple of Doctor Freuds. She gave each of their arms a warning pinch and turned her attention back to Charles White.

"It was a lucky guess," she explained and then added, "We don't *really* know your wife, Mr. White. It's just that we," she drew Sue and Nicole forward, "just happened to be here during yesterday's fire. We're the ones who tried to keep your wife from going into the building."

Eagerly the man took a step toward them. "That's what I want to talk to you about," he said. "My wife has only recently begun treatment for her disorder, and so things are still very out of control. The doctor isn't even sure how many identities we're dealing with yet. We do know about Barbie—and Barbara, of course—and another very timid personality, but..." he shook his head, "it's still all pretty mysterious. Barbara isn't even convinced she has a disorder. But... well... you saw Barbie yourself, so you know...it's true. The thing is I need to find out who started that fire. If it *was* Barbara—well, Barbie, actually—then I need to let the doctor and the police know."

He looked hopefully at Gina, but she shook her head apologetically. She felt sorry for him, but there was nothing she could tell him that would be of any help.

"I'm sorry," she said, "but we didn't see how the fire started. When we arrived, the building was already in flames. Your wife arrived after we did, and from the way she was acting, it didn't look like she knew what was going on. She was trying like crazy to get inside. She said she was trying to save her invention." Gina paused and eyed Charles White skeptically before continuing. "She said you were trying to steal it."

Charles heaved a huge sigh and shook his head wearily. "I know. But I'm not. When all this D.I.D. business started, I didn't know how it was going to affect Barbara's ability to work, so I tried to rush the patent through. For some reason, she decided I was trying to steal it. The patent application was filed two days ago—in Barbara's name."

Gina felt her body relax.

Sue glanced toward the car. "Where is your wife anyway?"

Charles looked over his shoulder. "Asleep in the back seat. Changing personalities tends to give her a migraine headache, and afterwards all she wants to do is sleep." He looked at Nicole. "That piece of chocolate was like a trigger, sending her into her Barbie personality. Chocolate always affects her that way. It's not a chemical response so much as an emotional trigger associated with the taste. That's why I was looking through the garbage. If Barbara had eaten chocolate before the fire, it might have caused Barbie to come out, and—as you saw—Barbie is a bit wild. I wouldn't put it past her to have started that fire."

"So what happens now?" Gina asked kindly.

Charles White shook his head. "It looks like she's going to have to be hospitalized for a while—until she can get her different identities under control. The doctor warned me that something like this might happen, but I didn't want to believe him. Barbara already thinks I'm against her." He sighed. "If she has to go into the hospital for treatment, she'll hate me for sure."

"Not once she starts to get better," Gina consoled him. "That's what you have to try to remember."

He nodded and glanced uneasily toward the car. Then he tried

MIGRAINES

Though no headache is fun, migraine headaches are the worst. Just ask any of the three million Canadians (17 percent of the population) who suffer from them. Once a migraine hits, it can leave the sufferer unable to function normally for up to three days! The weather, exposure to chemicals, eating certain foods—especially those containing caffeine—are all recognized triggers of migraines. And if you have others in your family who are prone to migraines, you may be more susceptible to these triggers.

There are three kinds of migraines: classic, common, and transformed. The classic migraine begins with a warning in the form of an aura (this is a visual, auditory, or sensory disturbance) followed by intense pain. The common migraine has no warning. The pain arrives so suddenly the victims might wonder if they had been struck by lightning. The transformed migraine is one that starts out as a tension headache (brought on by stress), which changes into a migraine.

Migraines can last for several hours or several days and go through four stages: prodrome, aura, headache, and postdrome. **Prodrome:** Almost 40 percent of migraine sufferers experience this phase, which occurs hours or days before a migraine attack and may involve mood swings, tiredness, stiffness in the neck, food cravings, chills, and water retention.
Aura: Though only 20 percent of the people who get migraines go through the aura stage, this warning phase is what makes a

migraine different from other types of headaches. It lasts from 15 minutes to an hour and may affect vision (in the form of blind spots, superimposed zigzag lines, distorted shapes, and flashes of light); hearing (ringing in the ears, or difficulty hearing); motor skills (speaking or understanding language); or sensory faculties (a greater or more subdued sensitivity to touch). Migraine sufferers may experience one or more of these symptoms. For some people, the aura can occur without being followed by the headache.

Headache: This is the worst part of the migraine and begins immediately after the aura has finished. It consists of a severe, throbbing pain that usually occurs on one side of the head, though it can affect the whole head. Often the pain is accompanied by nausea, vomiting, shaking, and extreme sensitivity to light and sound. The headache phase can last up to 72 hours.

Postdrome: In this last stage, the migraine sufferer is usually in a subdued mood, is unable to tackle big thinking tasks, finds it difficult to concentrate, is sluggish, irritable, tired, and weak. While a migraine runs its course, the sufferer is unable to function, and life is put on hold. The pain is caused by the swelling of blood vessels in the head, triggered by chemical changes in the body. Fortunately, there are medications to help prevent migraines as well as treat the symptoms.

to smile, but it looked more like a grimace. "Well, thank you for talking to me," he said. "Now I'd better call the doctor before Barbara wakes up." And without another word he trudged back to the car and drove off.

• • •

"That's so sad," Gina sighed, once the car was out of sight. "Bad things shouldn't happen to good people." Nicole and Sue nodded.

"We should think positively," Nicole reminded the others. "Every day, researchers are finding out more and more about the brain, including what causes mental illness."

Gina put on a cheery face. "You're absolutely right," she said, heading back toward the sidewalk. "It's just a matter of time. Science has given us so much to be thankful for. Sometimes we just take it for granted."

The girls walked in thoughtful silence for nearly a block, but as they waited at the intersection for the traffic signal to change, Sue said, "Did you know that by tracing the movement of underground water, speleologists are helping to prevent water pollution."

Nicole and Gina blinked at her, and then Nicole said, "And did *you* know that we have no idea what the heck you're talking about? What made you think of that? And what's a speleologist?"

Sue rolled her eyes. "You know," she grinned, "a spelunker."

"Well, that certainly clears everything up," Gina muttered irritably and then added, "NOT! Would you mind explaining what a spelunker is? And don't say speleologist, or I might have to hurt you."

Sue laughed and turned to Nicole. "I know *you* know what a spelunker is."

"I do?" Nicole's eyebrows jumped up in surprise.

The light turned to green, and the Science Squad began walking again.

"Sure," Sue said, stepping off the curb. "A *Spell*-unker is someone who flunks a spelling test."

Nicole groaned, and Gina said, "Very funny. Are you going to tell us what a spelunker is or aren't you?"

"Okay, okay," Sue sighed. "You guys are no fun at all. A spelunker —also known as a speleologist—is someone who studies and explores caves."

"Well, finally," Gina retorted snidely. "But couldn't these spelunker people call themselves something a little easier to remember like...I don't know...say...cavers, maybe?"

"Actually, that's exactly what they call themselves. And not only do they explore caves, but they study the rocks and crystals and plant and animal life inside them too. Cavers have uncovered all kinds of important stuff. They've even found 9000-year-old remains of prehistoric humans and animals."

Gina perked up. "Really?"

Sue nodded. "Yup."

"Well, I'll admit that's pretty interesting, but why, may I ask, are you telling us all this?" Gina said. "We were discussing brain disorders, and out of nowhere you start talking about caves!"

Sue shrugged. "I don't know. I just started thinking about our CAGIS event coming up next weekend, I guess."

"Is it next weekend?" Nicole gasped. "With the fire and the robberies and everything, I completely forgot about our CAGIS event!" And then her expression became clouded. "So why are you talking about caves? I thought we were going rock climbing."

"Caving *is* rock climbing—well, sort of," Sue explained. "It's just that you're climbing rocks on the *inside* instead of the outside. Cool, eh? You guys are going—right?"

"I wouldn't miss it," Gina said. "I'd like to find out more about the archaeological side of caves."

Sue nodded. "What about you, Nicole? You're coming, aren't you?"

Nicole chewed on her lip for a few seconds before answering. "I want to, but…"

"But what?" Sue demanded.

"You'll laugh at me," Nicole said quietly.

Gina and Sue stopped walking.

"No, we won't," Gina assured her, then added, "Will we, Sue?"

Sue seemed to be considering the question. "Well…" she stalled

PHOBIAS

A phobia is an intense, irrational fear of a specific situation or thing. A person might have a phobia about snakes, spiders, the number 13, flying, dancing, clocks—in fact, just about anything. And even though phobia sufferers know there is no good reason for them to be afraid, that doesn't stop them from having a panic attack when confronted by the thing that frightens them. They break into a sweat, their heart starts to pound, they become disoriented, and they hyperventilate. Some phobia sufferers freeze up, while others go wild.

Phobias affect more than one in 10 people, and though nobody can say for sure what causes them, they seem to strike more females than males and are often hereditary. Children sometimes experience great fear of certain things like dogs or electrical storms, but generally outgrow those fears. Phobias are different. They tend to develop in adolescence and early adulthood, and they don't go away.

until Gina stomped on her foot. "*Ow!* I was just kidding. You didn't have to cripple me. Of course we won't laugh."

"Well, I know a little bit about caves too," Nicole said, staring at the ground. "And what I know is that cave tunnels can be very narrow and low. And that wouldn't be good for me. You see, I'm not comfortable in tight places. They make me panicky. My brain knows I shouldn't be afraid, but I can't seem to help myself." She shrugged. "That's how it is when you have claustrophobia." ★

No one is clear about the causes of all phobias, but some phobias can be learned through classical conditioning (see p. 50).

If the thing that is feared can easily be avoided (as with Nicole's claustrophobia), treatment may not be necessary. But if a phobia gets in the way of everyday living, therapy should be sought. By gradually exposing the person to what scares them, the fear begins to fade. Seventy-five percent of phobia sufferers find this treatment helpful. Medication can be used in extreme or emergency situations, such as when a person with a phobia of flying absolutely has to get on a plane. Breathing exercises, hypnosis and a type of therapy called cognitive-behavioural are also used to help people with phobias.

MEMORY EXPERIMENT

Human beings experience three basic stages of memory. Sensory memory stays for a very short time. It's similar to looking at a light, then shutting your eyes. You still see the light for a split second. This is the type of memory we made use of in the animation experiment on p. 68. Working memory (formerly called short-term memory) can be thought of as the information you're thinking about at any given time (like remembering a phone number from a phone book). Long-term memory consists of knowledge and memories of experiences that may lie dormant and inactive for long periods of time but can be retrieved from your memory banks. Long-term memory has a huge storage capacity that many believe to be infinite (meaning that it can never become full). Any information to be remembered for a long period of time must enter each of these stages in order.

Many things that are in sensory memory or working memory never get encoded into long-term memory. So you won't be able to retrieve them at a later date. For example, if you look in the phone book for a number to make an immediate call, unless you keep rehearsing the number, chances are it won't be encoded in long-term memory. So if you need that phone number at a later date, you will probably have to look it up again. The amount of information you can keep in working memory is between five and nine items (that's why most phone numbers are that length). Would you like to test how good your working memory is? Try this experiment with friends and family to see who has the best working memory.

Materials:

* ✳ two placemats
* ✳ 10–20 small items (like a crayon, paper clip, candy, etc.)
* ✳ pencils and paper
* ✳ timer

Procedure:

1. Set five items randomly on the placemat. Make sure the person you are going to test is not in the room while you are setting up.
2. Cover the items with a second placemat.
3. Ask your test subject to come back into the room.
4. Remove the placemat covering the objects and allow the subject 60 seconds to memorize the objects.
5. After 60 seconds, put the placemat back on top of the object to hide them again and ask the subject to write down on a piece of paper as many of the items as she can remember.
6. Repeat this experiment with different objects, and each time add one more object (you started with five objects, next use six objects, then seven...)

When a person can no longer remember all the objects, her working memory capacity has been reached. The average person should remember anywhere from five to nine objects.

What Happened?

The important thing about working memory is that it has limited capacity, which means it can hold only a certain amount of information at one time. This is very important because if our brains could hold too much information in short-term storage, the system could become overloaded and break down.

The human brain is programmed to hold only a certain amount

of information at the sensory and working memory stage so we don't become overloaded. Information we pick up from our senses (sensory memory) moves to our working (short-term) memory. To keep information in our working memory, we repeat it over and over again so we don't forget it. The capacity of our working memory is limited. That is why most people would not be able to remember more than nine objects. If you remembered more than nine items, you have a great working memory!

More?

The same experiment can be done by reading words or numbers to your subjects to test their working memory. In this case, you would read to them five letters or numbers and ask them to say the words or numbers back to you, *but* in the reverse order. So if you read the numbers 1, 7, 5, 4, they would have to say 4, 5, 7, 1 back to you. This exercise tests another component of working memory.

10

Trapped!

About twenty girls turned out for the CAGIS event—including Nicole. A talk with her doctor, along with a dose of positive thinking from her friends, and the assurances of the caving staff that they would keep a close eye on the situation, convinced her to go along. With the help of therapy, Nicole's claustrophobia had been improving, and she knew she would kick herself later if she didn't at least try.

Though the cave system they were going to explore was located in a secluded woodland area, it was only a short drive from the city, and by the time the girls arrived they were more than a little excited. Their guides, Marta and Stephanie, met them in the parking lot and escorted them to the cave entrance.

While Stephanie helped the girls into their gear, Marta shielded her eyes from the sun and pointed toward a steep bank. "When you girls are ready," she told them, "we'll climb those rocks to the ledge up there. That's where the sinkhole is."

"Sinkhole?" someone questioned.

"Sorry," Marta grinned. "That's what we call the entrance to the cave. Sinkholes are created when carbon dioxide in rain becomes carbonic acid—that's kind of like the fizz in soft drinks—and it bores a hole through the rock. Actually, the entire cave is created that way. Once through the sinkhole, water keeps eating at the rock, forming underground streams that eventually create a network of tunnels—and that's our cave. So when you girls are all set, we'll go exploring."

Sue adjusted the chinstrap on her helmet and snapped it into place. "I can hardly wait to get going," she announced, hopping around. Feeling for the lamp mounted on her hard hat, she said, "I feel like a lighthouse."

"You'll get used to it," Gina told her as she fastened her own helmet and tied the laces of her boots. "It would be pretty tough to climb and carry a flashlight too."

"I'm boiling," Nicole complained, pulling at her layers of clothing. "It's almost 20° today, so why do we have to dress like it's the middle of winter?"

Sue fished her gloves from her jacket pocket and pulled them on. "Because it's not 20° inside the cave. Don't you remember what Marta said? The further in we go, the colder it gets. If we got lost or stuck inside a tunnel for any length of time, hypothermia could be a real problem."

A look of panic took over Nicole's face, and Gina quickly gave her hand a squeeze.

"Don't worry," she said, throwing Sue a dirty look. "That's not going to happen. You're going to be just fine."

• • •

Once on the ledge, Marta spoke to the girls again.

"Now remember the things I told you," she said. "Caving is fun and fascinating, but only as long as you obey the rules." She counted the regulations off on her fingers. "Number one—stay on the approved underground routes. In other words, stay with Stephanie and me. Don't go wandering off on your own. Number two—don't litter the cave or mark it up in any way. No garbage and no graffiti. Number three—don't disturb the plant or animal life. Number four—don't touch the cave formations. Look at everything. Take lots of pictures, *but don't touch*!" She looked around at everyone. "Are we clear?"

The girls all nodded.

"Good," Marta's expression relaxed into a smile. "Then let's get going."

Nicole watched as a number of the girls went down. If they could do it, she could too, she told herself logically. And besides, her friends were going to be with her. She nudged Sue and pointed to the sinkhole. "You're next."

She watched as her friend easily made the descent. Then she moved closer, took a deep breath, and prepared to enter the hole too, but Stephanie, who had stayed above ground to make sure everyone got into the cave safely, put out a hand to stop her.

"Wait until Sue is all the way down," she cautioned. "She'll be waiting for you at the bottom, and Gina will come right after you. If you think you won't be able to handle it, just shout, and you can come right back out."

Nicole nodded, and when Sue had finally touched down, she began her descent. The sinkhole wasn't as tight a fit as she had expected, and instead of being a straight drop, it was sloped—

minimizing the chance of a fall. And since the ridges carved into its walls by the eroding water provided solid places to put her hands and feet, the climb down was fairly easy, and before she knew it she was standing on the cave floor.

HYPOTHERMIA

Human beings are warm-blooded animals. This means that even if the temperature of our surroundings changes, our body temperature remains constant—usually 37°C (98.6°F). Any fluctuation (rise or fall) indicates a problem. A rise in body temperature (fever) is associated with illness, while a drop in temperature is the first sign that a person is experiencing hypothermia.

According to the Encarta encyclopaedia, hypothermia occurs when "body temperature falls drastically as a result of exposure to cold." This, in turn, stops the flow of blood to the surface of the body and slows processes such as breathing and digestion. This metabolic slowdown can be helpful to doctors performing certain medical procedures, but when hypothermia occurs accidentally, the results can be fatal. In fact, hypothermia is the leading cause of death for people involved in outdoor activities.

One of the more frightening characteristics of hypothermia is that it sneaks up on its victims, so that they are often not even aware they're in trouble. One of the first symptoms is violent, uncontrollable shivering. Though everyone knows shivering is

So far so good.

Nicole gave Stephanie the all-clear signal and looked around. Here in the entrance zone of the cave, she was standing in a puddle of sunlight, almost as if a spotlight were focused on her. Tufts of

a sign of cold, most people don't know that it happens only when the body's temperature is between 35° and 37°C. Once the body's temperature drops below 35°C, the shivering stops and the hypothermia victim will need medical treatment.

Symptoms of hypothermia include:
- uncontrolled shivering
- slow, slurred speech
- confusion and loss of memory
- clumsiness
- overwhelming weariness
- drowsiness—*Sleeping can be fatal!*

All these things indicate the body is shutting down, and if immediate treatment isn't begun, death is inevitable. However, warming should be slow and gradual, using blankets and other similar methods so that the body temperature doesn't increase more than two degrees an hour. Anything more could cause the person's heart to stop working. In cases where the person has lost consciousness, medical treatment should be sought.

moss, grass, and other straggly plants she didn't know by name poked out of nearby crevices. As she watched, a large grey spider scuttled across the rock face and disappeared into a crack. There were probably other little critters lurking in the corners too, she decided, remembering what Stephanie and Marta had said about above-ground animals living in cave entrances.

Anxiously, Nicole peered deeper into the cavern. The daylight didn't extend far, and where two tunnels branched off—not five metres away, dusky shadows clung eerily to the walls. A shiver ran through her. That must be the beginning of the twilight zone. And beyond that was the dark zone where there was absolutely no light at all. She gulped. Then she reached up to the light on her helmet for reassurance and moved on to where Sue was standing with Marta and the rest of the CAGIS members.

• • •

Half an hour into their explorations, Nicole felt herself starting to relax. It was dark, but in a way that was a good thing. Nicole wasn't afraid of the dark, and the blackness had a way of hiding the spaces that were small. And there was so much to think about and look at, that she was able to push her anxiety to the back of her mind—mostly, anyway.

Just navigating the tunnels was a challenge. Some of them were several storeys tall while others were much lower and narrower, so that the girls were forced to crawl on their hands and knees or squeeze through sideways. These were the times the guide stayed with her and her friends kept her talking to keep her mind off her claustrophobia. Sometimes they found themselves climbing up a wall to get to the next chamber; other times they had to climb down. How Marta and Stephanie knew where they were going amazed Nicole. She was drawing a map of the cave's layout, but even so she was fairly certain that if she became separated from the group, she would be stuck inside the cave forever. The mere possibility made her shudder.

Don't think about that, she scolded herself. Just concentrate on how awesome the place is. And it was true. The caverns and tunnels were spectacular. Though they weren't filled with water any more, there were signs of water everywhere. Often it just dripped, echoing hollowly as it splattered onto the cave floor, but there were places where it flowed freely down the rock walls into pools, and in one cavern there was actually a waterfall!

Even in the parts of the cave where there was no water at all, there was still evidence that it had been there once. Calcite deposits formed by the action of the carbonic acid on the rock had created an underground museum of amazingly beautiful formations—pots of calcite pearls, crystalline cave blisters, moonmilk, cave coral called popcorn, and, of course, stalagmites and stalactites. Nicole had never been able to remember which was which until Stephanie told her to think of the calcite icicles as ants in her pants. *When the mites go up, the tites go down,* she'd said.

If it just weren't so cold! Gina had certainly been right about the temperature change.

"I'm freezing," Nicole complained when the group stopped to examine the bones of a 5000-year-old marmot. "I can barely feel my toes."

Gina shook her head. "Will you make up your mind?" she said. "One minute you're boiling, the next you're freezing. I think you need to get your thermostat checked."

Sue laughed and snapped a photograph of the marmot bones. "I sure hope these pictures turn out. It's awfully dark in here."

"No kidding," Nicole frowned. Her partly drawn map was propped on her knee, and she was trying to write on it, but between

CAVE FORMATIONS

Caves are formed through the erosion of soluble rocks such as limestone. (Soluble means capable of being dissolved.) Limestone is a stone made up of a mineral called calcite, or scientifically referred to as calcium carbonate ($CaCO_3$). Falling rain absorbs carbon dioxide from the air. As it hits the ground and seeps through the soil, it becomes slightly acid, so that when it reaches the limestone, the acid dissolves tiny particles of the rock and carries them downward.

Water entering the cave tends to cling to the roof in droplets. As these droplets evaporate, calcium carbonate is precipitated (meaning it separates into a solid from the water solution). These tiny crystals of calcite brought into caves drop by drop become beautiful icicle-like shapes.

Stalactites and stalagmites are examples of this process. These icicle-like formations are created by constantly dripping water. This water contains minerals accumulated through the erosion process, and over time the minerals deposited by the drips build up. Stalagmites grow from the ground up, and stalactites grow from the roof down. To understand how this process works, try the experiment at the end of this chapter. You'll have to be patient, though, because it will take several days to get full results.

her shivering and the fluttering of the lamp on her helmet, she wasn't having much luck. "I'm trying to make a map of the cave, but I'll never get it labelled properly in this light," she complained.

"Let me take a look," Gina said, fiddling with Nicole's helmet. "It's just a loose connection. There—it should be fine now."

"Come on, everyone," Stephanie rounded the girls up. "There are some interesting fish fossils in the next chamber. Then it's just a short walk through a twisty tunnel, a climb up another one, a stroll back along the main passage, and we're back to the sinkhole."

The next chamber was the biggest they'd been in during their explorations, and its walls were gnarled and sculpted from thousands of years of water coursing through it. On her map Nicole drew in the five tunnels feeding into the chamber, and again she marvelled that Marta and Stephanie could remember which tunnel was which. Along with the fossils Stephanie had promised them, the girls were treated to an alcove framed in stalagmites and stalactites that gave Nicole the creepy feeling she was gazing into a shark's mouth. And then to top things off, there was the sudden hollow thumping of wings, and everyone went scurrying for cover as a dozen bats swooped toward their heads.

• • •

The girls were still chattering giddily about the flying mammals when they got back to the sinkhole.

"That was so cool!" Sue bubbled enthusiastically when she was once more safely above ground. "I am totally hooked. I *have to* do this again!"

"I liked it too," Gina grinned. "I wouldn't mind exploring some other caves. It was sort of like an archaeological dig, except there was no digging."

BATS

Bats are mammals, so they are warm-blooded, their young are born live, and they are suckled by their mothers. What makes bats different from other mammals is their ability to fly. Their wings are made of skin, which fold up tightly to their bodies when not in use.

Bats can live in all kinds of climates as long as the weather isn't too hot or too cold. Scientists have identified nearly 1000 different types of bats throughout the world. In Canada alone, there are 19 different varieties, the most common of which is the little brown bat. When sleeping, it seems quite tiny, weighing a mere eight grams. Yet when it is in flight, its 22-centimetre wingspan makes it seem much larger.

Bats are basically nocturnal creatures, so most of their activity—mainly hunting—takes place after dark. In tropical climates, bats are known to eat fish, fruit, and, yes, even blood! But in Canada, bats stick pretty much to a diet of insects. The little brown bat can catch as many as 600 mosquitoes in one hour. While insect-eating birds tend to catch their prey right in their mouths, bats are more likely to swoop them up in their wings first.

The expression "blind as a bat" is misleading because bats actually have very good vision. Nevertheless, they prefer to hunt using a technique called echolocation. (That's like a Doppler Effect; see p. 73.) By emitting a high-pitched call and noting the difference in the sound when it echoes back, bats locate their supper. With a few exceptions, these calls can't be heard by human ears.

Bats live in large colonies, roosting upside down in trees, on cliff sides, in caves, and in buildings such as barns. Flight is just a matter of releasing their toehold and opening their wings. The wings of bats are very interesting because they are not like the wings of birds. The wings of bats are in fact hands! If you look at a bat wing, you will see long thin bones; these are really elongated fingers covered by a thin layer of skin stretched over each side. The bat's arms run along the top edge of the wings. Scientists often refer to bats as being "hand-winged," and these special wings make bats the only mammal capable of flight.

Females have just one pup per year, usually sometime in June, and by three weeks, the babies are flying. Bats that live in colder climates generally migrate and hibernate during the winter.

"What about you, Ni..." Sue's voice trailed off as she looked around for her friend. "Nicole?" Then she looked quizzically at Gina. "Where's Nicole?"

Gina peered around the group of girls already above ground. "There," she pointed to a curly-haired girl in a red jacket.

Sue looked.

"That's not Nicole," she said, worry suddenly filling her voice.

Gina looked again. "Oh, my gosh! You're right. That girl was behind me the whole way back, and I just assumed it was Nicole." She took a deep breath. "Don't panic. Not everybody is up yet. Maybe Nicole is with Marta."

Anxiously, the two girls stood by the sinkhole and watched as the rest of the CAGIS group emerged from the cave. But when Marta climbed out too, they knew something was wrong.

Sue swallowed hard and grabbed Gina's arm. "Nicole must still be in the cave." ★

CAVE FORMATIONS EXPERIMENT

Materials:
- ✻ two glass jars
- ✻ a saucer
- ✻ a piece of wool or cotton yarn, string, or thick thread, approximately 50 centimetres long
- ✻ baking soda or Epsom salts (these represent dissolved minerals)
- ✻ very warm water
- ✻ screws or nails

Procedure:
1. Fill the glass jars with very warm water and add as much baking soda or Epsom salts to each container as will dissolve.

2. Arrange the jars so that they are far enough apart to fit the saucer between them.

3. Tie a screw or nail to each end of the string. These will act as weights. Now place one end of the string into each jar so that the end hangs into the solution but doesn't touch the bottom of the jar. The string should sag in the middle where it goes across the saucer.

4. Leave it for a few days.

What Happened?

Capillary action caused the solution to soak the string and travel along its length. The water solution soaked the string, but while the solution was on the string, the water evaporated, leaving the mineral to crystallize.

More?

Different minerals form different crystal patterns. Those created using Epsom salts are different from the ones made by baking soda. In the same way, formations will change if the water is deposited differently. What would happen if the water dripped down something flat like a wall or was allowed to flow in a snaky pattern? What would happen if the evaporation process were speeded up? Can you think of ways to change the types of formations created?

CAPILLARY ACTION

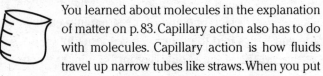

You learned about molecules in the explanation of matter on p. 83. Capillary action also has to do with molecules. Capillary action is how fluids travel up narrow tubes like straws. When you put a clear straw in juice, you will notice that the juice moves up to a higher level in the straw than it is in the glass. The narrower the straw or tube in the glass, the higher the juice moves. If you put a piece of string in the juice, or in water as in the previous experiment, the water moves a very long way along the string because the string isn't all material. There are air pockets inside the string that create very thin tubes for the water to move up, the way it did in the straw. But since these tubes are so thin, the water can move farther along the string than it can in the straw.

The reason this happens is adhesion. Adhesion is a force of attraction between molecules of different substances (forces between molecules are called intermolecular forces). There are also intermolecular forces between molecules of the same substance. For example, there are weak forces of attraction between water molecules called hydrogen bonds. In capillary action, the water or juice moves up the straw because the forces of adhesion between the water molecules and plastic molecules of the straw are stronger than the forces of attraction between the molecules of water (the hydrogen bonds). Capillary action is also how plants pull water upward through their stems to their leaves and flowers.

11

Race Against Time

When the bats had swooped down from the ceiling of the cave, sending everyone diving to the floor, Nicole had been busy with her pencil and paper, adding the layout of the cavern to her map. But it wasn't an easy task. This particular part of the cave was quite large, and its odd shape and the numerous tunnels exiting from it into the blackness made it a challenge for Nicole to record with any accuracy. Of course, having to use her knee as a drawing table didn't help. Neither did the fact that her fingers were so cold they could barely hold the pencil. Her bulky gloves made sketching impossible, so Nicole had stuffed them into the pocket of her jacket and, except when she was climbing, that's where they stayed.

So when she hit the ground to avoid the bats, her fingers were so stiff with cold they dropped both the pencil and the paper. Nicole managed to grab hold of the partially drawn map as it fluttered to the cave floor, but the pencil rolled beneath an overhang of rock. She had to crawl on her stomach to retrieve it, and by the time she had backed out again and regained her feet, she was alone. The group had moved on.

But which way had it gone?

Nicole squinted toward the various tunnels, trying to see a glimmer of light that would indicate the route she should follow, but each one looked as dark and uninviting as the next. She cocked her head to one side and listened. She could hear voices—though barely. She hurried toward the sound.

But there were two tunnels branching off from the cavern at this point, and Nicole couldn't tell which one the voices were coming from. Sounds had a strange way of bouncing off the walls, and a noise that seemed to be in front of her might actually be coming from behind. The thought of choosing the wrong tunnel and ending up in one that narrowed to nothing and locked her in was enough to keep her standing right where she was. By the time she thought to call out, the voices had disappeared altogether.

Nicole stuffed her pencil and paper into her pocket. But after that, she was unsure what to do. She knew she should be frightened at being alone in the cave but, strangely enough, she was quite calm. Everything seemed to be happening in slow motion, so that she felt as if she was walking through a dream. There was no hurry, no worry, no panic. No doubt her brain was as frozen as the rest of her, she decided. Her shivering had become so violent that her teeth had started chattering. Her hands and feet were numb now too. Nicole stomped her boots to get the blood circulating, but it was like banging blocks of wood. She felt nothing. Her feet might as well have belonged to someone else.

Nicole's eyes travelled back and forth between the mouths of the tunnels. Perhaps she should just choose one and take her chances. Or, she thought some more, maybe she should stay where she was and wait. Surely her friends would realize she was missing, and the group would come back to look for her. Yes, that was a better idea. She would wait.

Nicole hugged herself against the cold, and looked around. With just the one small torch on her helmet to light the cavern, it was much more dark and daunting than when the entire group had been there. A small rainbow of light lit the area immediately in front of her, but beyond that, murky shadows gave way to an inky abyss, and if Nicole had been more alert, she would have imagined all kinds of scary monsters lurking in the blackness beyond.

She yawned. She was so very tired.

• • •

Emergency crews and equipment had arrived, and the girls from CAGIS moved down the embankment, away from the sinkhole, so that the rescue team had more room to manoeuvre. Gina and Sue clung to each other, watching anxiously as Marta, along with two men, started back down into the cave with ropes and blankets and a collapsible stretcher. The girls felt so helpless. All they could do was watch, wait, and worry.

"How could I not notice she wasn't with us?" Sue wailed. "What kind of friend am I?"

"Don't go blaming yourself," Gina comforted her. "I should have been paying more attention too. But I was too engrossed in the cave."

"That huge cavern with all the stalagmites and stalactites was the last place I remember seeing Nicole," Sue said. "I was right behind her when we entered it, and then she started working on her map, and I started looking around, and we lost track of each other. And then there was all the commotion with the bats."

"That's right. I didn't see her after that either," Gina agreed. "I thought I had, but it was really somebody else with the same jacket."

"What could have happened to her?" Sue couldn't keep the worry out of her voice. "What if she got lost or knocked out or something!"

CARTOGRAPHY

A map is a two-dimensional (flat) representation (picture) of a specific place. Generally maps take an overhead view of things (a bird's-eye view). Maps are usually drawn to scale so that they keep the same proportions as the actual locations they represent. Maps may be drawn for small areas (the furniture arrangement in a room) or very large areas (world shipping routes), and will appear quite different depending on the information they are trying to convey.

Anyone who has ever gone on a car trip will be familiar with road maps—those large, awkward, folded sheets of criss-crossing lines and tiny writing that travellers rely on to find their way around strange cities. But maps can do much more than simply help a person get from one place to another. Maps can show climatic zones (like weather maps with different temperatures), migration patterns, earthquake hazard areas, the rivers of the world, the location of mineral deposits—even the distribution of this book, which would help the publisher meet the future needs of readers.

The process of making maps is called cartography, and people who take part in this process are called cartographers.

Stephanie must have overheard her, because she walked over and put a reassuring hand on Sue's shoulder. "Now don't get yourself all worked up," she told her. "I'm sure Nicole is fine. If she doesn't panic and if she remembers the things Marta said before we went into the cave, she'll be okay. I'm sure—"

Archaeological evidence indicates that people have been making maps for a very long time. In fact, scientists have found the remains of a clay map from Babylon dating back to 1000 BC! Because early people's knowledge of the world was minimal, and their expertise with mathematics was limited, the first maps weren't always very accurate. But, as early as 200 BC—long before Christopher Columbus set out to prove the world was round or Ferdinand Magellan circumnavigated it (sailed around the world)—the Greeks knew the earth was a sphere and were even able to accurately calculate its circumference (the distance around the world). In the 1500s, a cartographer named Mercator invented a map that could show the round earth on a flat surface. This was a great help to sailors. Then in the 19th century, mapmaking became even more sophisticated when Greenwich, England, was established as the prime meridian (where the longitude is 0) and the adoption of the metric system provided a universal language for map scale.

Today, thanks to advanced mathematics, aerial photography, computers, and space science, maps are more accurate than ever. And consequently a lot more useful.

Stephanie's sentence was interrupted by a static-riddled voice on the walkie-talkie.

"Any sign of her yet?" Stephanie said into the communicator.

In spite of the static, the girls caught the answer from down inside the cave. "Not yet. Keep your fingers crossed that's she's in that cavern. We're almost there."

• • •

Nicole wasn't sure when it had happened, but she wasn't shivering any more. Perhaps the cave was warming up, she thought groggily. She seemed to have lost all sense of time, and she had no idea how long she'd been in the cave. Using the wall for balance, she dragged herself to her feet. She'd take another look down the tunnels to see if anyone was coming.

But once upright, she couldn't remember which way to go. Beyond the meagre puddle of light provided by the torch on her helmet, she could see nothing and couldn't think which way was which.

"Eenie, meenie, minie, moe," she giggled, and then stumbled off across the cavern, mindless of where she was going. She felt like she was wearing huge clown shoes, staggering and tripping with every step.

And then she lost her balance completely and went down hard, banging her head on the floor of the cave. It wasn't enough to hurt her, but it jarred a connection on the torch wiring of her helmet, and the light sputtered a couple of times before finally dying altogether.

Suddenly it was absolutely dark. In fact, it was so thick, Nicole felt as if she was wrapped in it. She lifted her head and blinked into the blackness. Her eyelids felt so heavy. She couldn't remember ever being this tired in her whole life.

Nicole laid her head on her arms. Since she couldn't see to go anywhere now, she might as well have a little rest.

"Nicole! Nicole! Nicole, are you here?" Marta called, as she aimed the torch's beam along the tunnel walls and floor ahead of her. She and the other two members of the rescue team were moving as quickly as the narrow twists and turns of the cave would allow. Finally they were back at the entrance to the cavern.

"This is the last place anyone remembers seeing her," Marta told the fellows with her. "If she isn't in here, then we're going to have to check all the tunnels running off it, and if she's taken one of them, we might not find her in time. According to her friends, she was already cold. We could be looking at hypothermia here."

As they entered the body of the cavern, the three rescuers spread out to cover more ground.

"Nicole!" they called, as their flashlights searched every corner and crevice. "Nicole!" they kept calling. But there was no answer.

And then, two-thirds of the way through the cavern, off to one side in a sheltered alcove, they found her. ★

GLOBE TO MAP EXPERIMENT

The earth is a sphere; however, maps representing it are flat. Changing a globe into a map seems like an impossible thing to accomplish, and yet that is exactly what cartographers try to do. By shining a light at different angles onto a clear globe of the earth, mapmakers can project images of that globe onto flat surfaces. These are called projections, and though they aren't perfect, they provide the most accurate maps cartographers have so far been able to create. Depending on how the light is pointed at the globe and how the flat surface is arranged to receive the projection, the maps will vary. There are three main types of projections: planar,

Mercator, and conical. From these basic three, many other projections have been developed.

To understand how distortions develop when the earth is represented on a flat surface, try this experiment.

THE SUN

Though it is a bright, warm day outside the cave, the Science Squad finds that the temperatures underground are freezing, and without artificial lighting, it is completely black. That is because the cave is untouched by the sun's rays.

The sun makes all life on earth possible. It has the power to destroy us with its intense heat, but without it we would freeze to death.

The sun is actually a star. It was formed approximately 4.5 billion years ago, and scientists estimate that it will last another 5 billion years. It is the centre of our solar system—about 150 million kilometres from earth, and though it is only average in size as far as stars go, it would take 1.3 million earths to fill it!

The sun is literally a ball of fire. Science estimates that temperatures at its core are 15 million degrees Celsius. The surface is much cooler—only around 6000°C. The outer atmosphere

Materials:

* ✳ an orange (one with a fairly thin skin is best)
* ✳ a felt marker
* ✳ paring knife or craft knife
* ✳ a pencil
* ✳ a ruler or other straight edge
* ✳ paper

(made up of the photosphere, chromosphere, transitional region, and corona) reaches temperatures from 10 to 22 million degrees Celsius. (Obviously, sunscreen is a must!)

The sun is mainly composed of two gases: 75 percent hydrogen and 25 percent helium. The sun is constantly changing huge quantities of hydrogen into helium, a reaction that releases approximately five million tonnes of energy into the solar system every second. It is this energy that allows life on Earth to flourish.

However, the very sun that gives us life will one day destroy the earth. The sun is slowly using up its supply of hydrogen, and when that happens, it will start to change drastically. It will swell up and swallow our planet. Eventually the sun will collapse.

Procedure:

In this experiment, the orange is going to represent the earth, and by peeling it, you are going to turn it into a map.

1. To begin, use the felt marker to draw lines of longitude (vertical lines) and latitude (horizontal lines) on the orange. These lines are used on maps for navigational purposes. *Note:* Longitude lines intersect or cross one another at the top and bottom of the orange. Latitude lines do not intersect. See the diagram.

2. Using the knife, cut through the skin of the orange along one of the longitude lines. Make the cut down one side of the orange only. You want to get the peel off in one piece, and if you cut all the way around, that won't be possible. Now cut through the skin partway up and down each of the other lines of longitude. This will help you peel the orange without ripping the skin. (See the broken line in the diagram.)

3. Now carefully peel the orange, making sure to keep the skin in one piece.

4. Place the skin of the orange onto a piece of paper so that it lies flat. You may need to lengthen the cuts along the longitude lines to do this. Notice the shape of the peel.

5. Trace the outline of the peel onto the paper.

6. Lay the ruler on top of the peel so that its edge is on a latitude or longitude line. With your pencil, extend that line onto the paper in both directions. Repeat the process for all the other lines. See the diagram.

7. Remove the orange skin from the paper and use the ruler to draw a box around the orange peel outline.

8. Eat the orange!

What Happened?

Could you get the orange skin to lie completely flat? Why or why not? Do the lines of longitude and latitude look different on the flat surface than they did on the orange? Why do you think that is? Observe the space within the box but outside the orange peel outline. How might that distort a map?

Because an orange, like the earth, is round, the middle part is larger than the top and bottom parts when you lie it flat. If you were going to make a map in the shape of a rectangle, the top and bottom parts of the earth would have to be stretched to make it fit the page. This would make the upper and lower parts of the earth look wider than they really are.

More?

Try the experiment again. This time, draw a few continents on the orange before you peel it. Make sure to include Antarctica. What happens to the shape of the continents when the peel is laid flat? What happened to Antarctica? Would this be a useful map for navigation? Give reasons for your opinion.

12

Journey to the Tropics

"What time is it?" Sue demanded anxiously.

Gina didn't even bother looking at her watch. She merely sighed. "About forty seconds later than it was the last time you asked. For goodness sake, Sue, try to relax a little."

"Relax! How can I? My best friend in the whole world is trapped in an underground cave, slowly freezing to death, and you expect me to relax?"

Gina lowered her eyes and chewed on her lip.

"I'm sorry. I didn't mean to bark at you. I know you're worried about Nicole—I am too—but working yourself into a fit isn't going to help. Those people looking for her are professionals. They'll find her and bring her back safely. I know they will." Then she offered Sue an encouraging smile.

"I sure hope you're right," Sue replied, but the furrows in her forehead didn't ease up, and she began pacing mechanically back and forth once more.

Gina spied Stephanie and went to see if there was any news.

"Have they found her?" she asked anxiously.

Stephanie no sooner finished shaking her head than the communicator in her hand began to crackle. Quickly, she put it to her ear, grimacing at the heavy static spewing from it.

"Say again," she spoke into the transmitter. "You're breaking up. I repeat—you're breaking up. Say again."

Another explosion of harsh static filled the air, and Gina and Stephanie listened intently to make sense of it. But it was no use. It was impossible to decipher what the fuzzy voice was saying.

There was a pause and then another grating wave of static, but Gina did catch the last words of that transmission.

"...coming up," the voice had said.

Gina quickly turned to Stephanie. "Does that mean they've found her?"

Stephanie took a deep breath before replying. "I sure hope so."

• • •

When the rescue crew discovered Nicole, she was sitting on the cave floor with her back against the wall—and she was singing. As weary as she was, she knew she couldn't allow herself to sleep. If she fell asleep that could be the end, and Nicole was still lucid enough to know she didn't want to die. It had taken all her willpower to drag herself back to a sitting position, but she had done it. She had even managed to wrestle her gloves from her jacket pocket and put them on.

And that's when she'd heard the voices calling her name. At first, Nicole had thought she was imagining them. She was probably hallucinating. But the voices seemed to be getting closer, and that gave Nicole hope. She'd tried to answer, but she was so weak she couldn't manage anything more than a whisper. She was just going to have to wait—and pray—for them to find her.

In the meantime, she had to stay awake.

So she started to sing. *Row, row, row your boat* was the only thing she could think of, but at least she knew all the words. Besides, it didn't matter what she sang. The important thing was to stay awake.

"Merrily, merrily, merrily, merrily..." she mouthed the words soundlessly to the wall of blackness in front of her.

Wait a minute. All of a sudden it didn't seem quite so dark. Nicole could see muddy shadows in the distance—to her left.

Call out! The thought pushed itself through the fog of her mind.

"...merrily, merrily, merrily..." she breathed hoarsely.

The shadows were becoming sharper—and closer. And then Nicole saw a shimmer of light...and then another and another.

She lifted her arm weakly to attract attention to herself, but it fell limply back into her lap.

Merrily, merrily... her head sang, but her lips no longer moved.

"Nicole! Nicole! Nicole, where are you?" Marta shouted on the other side of the torch light.

I'm here, Nicole's mind cried out. *Please find me!*

• • •

The rescue team didn't waste any time taking control. The instant they discovered Nicole huddled in the alcove of the cavern, they swung into action, using their equipment and knowledge to battle her hypothermia. And the whole time they worked, they talked softly to her, asking her questions, assuring her she was going to be fine, and making sure she didn't fall asleep.

LARYNX

 Humans are able to produce sound with the aid of a handy-dandy little body part called the larynx or voice box. This is located in the throat, right at the entrance to the trachea (the tube that takes the air we breathe to our lungs) and the esophagus (the passageway to our stomachs).

You've probably seen a bony bump called an Adam's apple on some men's necks. This is the larynx. It's not very big, only about five centimetres high, but it carries out a very big job. It allows us to project sound.

Actually, the larynx performs three important tasks. It regulates breathing, it protects the windpipe or trachea, and it produces sound.

The larynx is a ring of cartilage (tough, flexible tissue found in joints, noses, and external ears), and inside it are muscles known as the vocal cords. During breathing, the muscles pull apart to allow air to pass through into the trachea, but when we speak, the vocal cords rub together and vibrate to produce sound (see p. 25 for an explanation of sound waves). What we do with that sound is left up to our tongue, lips, and throat.

The vocal cords in the larynx are controlled by something called the vagus nerve. This nerve can be damaged by a number of things, including trauma, and can cause a person to lose his or her voice.

They checked her breathing and her heart rate. They flashed a light into her eyes. They wrapped her in blankets and moved her gently onto the stretcher they'd brought with them. They inserted an IV into her arm. Most of this Nicole was too groggy to notice, but the one thing that did catch her attention was the mask they placed over her face. The instant they did that, a wonderful wave of warmth began to fill her lungs, and somehow she knew she was going to be all right. Everything was going to be okay.

It wasn't long before Nicole and her rescuers were on the move. The men carried the stretcher while Marta juggled the IV and kept Nicole talking. All Nicole had to do was float through the tunnels of the cave on her stretcher. How her rescuers managed to manoeuvre the narrow pathways without jostling or dropping her, Nicole had no idea, but when she thought about it afterwards she couldn't recall a single bump. And she hadn't felt the slightest twinge of claustrophobia either. All she could remember was how glorious it had felt to breathe that warm, moist air.

And the next thing she knew, she was squinting into the bright sunlight.

• • •

Nicole spent the next two days in the hospital—as a precaution— but when she arrived home, she was as good as new. Nevertheless, her parents insisted she take it easy for a little while longer. But after seventy-two straight hours of inactivity, Nicole couldn't stand it any longer, and her mother and father finally relented and let her join her friends.

As the Science Squad walked lazily along the woodland paths near Nicole's home, they relived their exciting caving adventure one more time. Of course, Sue had photographs, and each one prompted myriad memories.

The girls stopped beside an old dilapidated fence to study the snapshots more closely, and Nicole perched on a rotted post in a dappled pool of sunlight. She peered up at the sun winking through the thick canopy of leaves above her.

"Whew! It's warm," she said, flapping her T-shirt for relief.

Gina laughed. "I never thought I'd hear you complaining about the heat ever again."

Nicole smiled. "Me neither. But I'm sure glad I can. Hypothermia isn't something I ever want to experience again, thank you."

"I guess not," Sue said, not bothering to look up from a patch of grass she was poking through. "I wouldn't want to experience it even once!"

"What are you looking for?" Gina asked.

"Nothing," Sue shrugged. "I'm just looking."

"You know," Nicole said, changing the subject, "it seems like a lot of stuff has happened lately."

"What do you mean?" Gina asked.

"Well, I was just thinking about how busy we've been the last few weeks. It started with that robbery at the aquarium—remember? And then we caught the thief—"

"Thieves," Gina corrected her.

"Right. Thieves," Nicole nodded. "Then there was the fire that we discovered, which led to us meeting that strange lady with the personality disorder. And then I got trapped in the cave."

"You're right," Gina agreed. "That is a lot of excitement. *Too much,* if you ask me. And I, for one, am ready for a nice long stretch of boredom."

The words were no sooner out of her mouth than Sue called from across the clearing. She was waving something that looked like a wallet. "Hey, you guys, look what I found. It's somebody's passport."

Hurrying over for a closer look, Nicole elbowed Gina and grinned. "Did you just say something about boredom?"

HEAT EXPERIMENT

Because heat is so vital to our survival, it is important that we understand where to get it and how to make the most of it when we find it. Heat is a moving thing. For instance, it can

---

CONTROLLING BODY TEMPERATURE

Cold-blooded animals are able to adapt their body temperature to their surroundings—more or less—while warm-blooded animals must maintain a constant body temperature to live. Even a five or six degree change up or down can lead to death. That's why Nicole suffered from hypothermia. Being in the cold cave for an extended period of time weakened her ability to maintain a constant body temperature.

You might argue that polar bears are mammals too, and they survive in far colder conditions than Nicole experienced. That's true. However, polar bears are a lot bigger than Nicole, and studies have shown that smaller mammals lose body heat far more quickly than larger ones. Also, polar bears have very thick fur and a considerable layer of fat beneath their skin to help insulate them. The problem for them arises when outside

move from one solid object to another. This movement is called conduction. Heat can also flow from a warm liquid into a cold one. This is called convection. And finally, it can move in waves through space in much the same way as sound and light do. This is called radiation.

To understand how conduction, convection, and radiation work, try the following activities.

temperatures get too warm. Unable to lower their body temperature at a rapid enough rate, they must seek an external method of cooling off, and a dip in the Arctic Ocean works nicely.

Aside from hunkering down in front of a fire or taking a refreshing dip in the ocean, mammals rely on a number of internal processes to regulate their body temperature thermostats. For instance, simply moving can affect temperature. The contraction of muscles creates heat. If you've ever shovelled snow on a winter day, you'll know that's true. It doesn't take long to warm up once you start heaving the white stuff around. Shivering helps generate heat in the same way, while sweating and panting act as cooling mechanisms by releasing heat through water.

The process of burning food creates heat too, and so does changing the direction of blood flow. Without realizing it, that's what we do when we stamp our feet or rub our hands together.

Materials:
* two glasses or cups
* very warm tap water and cold tap water
* thermometer (optional)
* an article of clothing from your dresser
* an article of clothing straight from the dryer
* toaster

Procedure:
1. Fill a glass halfway with cold water, and use your thermometer or your sense of touch to assess the temperature of the water.
2. Half fill a second glass with very warm (but not hot) water.
3. Now pour the warm glass of water into the cold glass of water and assess the temperature of the full glass of water.
4. Place a folded article of clothing onto a flat surface, noting the temperature.
5. Take an article of clothing that has just been heated in the dryer, fold it and place on top of the first item of clothing.
6. Leave for about five minutes and then remove the top item of clothing and place your hand on the bottom one.
7. Holding one hand about 15 centimetres above the bread slots, push the lever down on a plugged-in toaster. Be very careful not to hold your hand too close to the toaster.

What Happened?
What did you notice about the temperature of the cold water when you added the hot water to it? Did it become warmer in just some places or all the way through? Why do you think that happened?

When you removed the article of dryer clothing from the dresser drawer clothing, did you notice a change in the warmth of the dresser clothing? What method of heat movement does this activity illustrate? Feel the underside of the dresser clothing. Does it feel the same as the topside? How do you account for that?

When you pushed down the lever of the toaster, was there a change in the warmth of your hand? Slowly move your hand away. What do you notice about the heat? What conclusion can you draw about heat radiation?

Whenever there is a temperature difference between two objects, liquids or gases, heat energy is transferred from the hotter to the cooler place. This increases the internal energy of the cooler molecules, raising their temperature and reducing the energy of the hotter molecules, lowering their temperature. This process continues until the temperature is the same, which is called thermal equilibrium. In the first experiment, when a hot liquid was mixed with a cold liquid, the heat was transferred by convection. If you had two glasses of water the same size, one with a temperature of 10°C, the other with a temperature of 20°C, the temperature of the mixed glass would be 15°C. In the second experiment, because the heat was transferred from one solid object to the other, heat was transferred by conduction. In the last experiment, the toaster was warming the air by radiation.

More?

Think about the idea of hypothermia again. Often when two people find themselves caught in the cold, they huddle together for warmth. Think about what you've just learned about the movement of heat to explain why this works.

Acknowledgements

The fictitious characters of "Science Sue" and her original Science Squad were introduced in the first published newsletter of the Canadian Association for Girls In Science (CAGIS). Modelled after actual CAGIS members, these girls were interested in all aspects of science, technology, engineering, and mathematics. In 1999, the founding president of CAGIS, Larissa Vingilis-Jaremko, and Dr. Evelyn Vingilis conceived of developing stories, based on the Science Squad, where the Squad used their science to solve mysteries. A grant from the Ministry of Energy, Science and Technology of Ontario provided the support to produce the Science Squad Webisodes, which formed the basis of this book.

References

About Homework Help. 2002. Police Technology and Forensic Science. Web site: About Homework Help. URL: http://inventors. about.com/library/inventors/blforensic.htm. Article read: May 26, 2002.

Arai Helmet Europe. 2001. What happens with the Helmet during an Impact? Web site: Arai Helmet Europe. URL: http://www.araihelmet -europe.com/tecs/impact.htm. Article read on May 10, 2002.

Arnett, W. 2001. The Sun. Web site: The Nine Planets. URL: http://www. nineplanets.org/sol.html. Article read: June 9, 2002.

Bourne, L. and B. Ekstrand. 1971. *Psychology: Its Principles and Meanings*. Holt, Rinehart & Winston, New York.

Centre for the Communication of Science. Einstein's Brain. Web site: Centre for the Communication of Science. URL: http://www. moray.ac.uk/css/einstein.htm. Article read: May 10, 2002.

Chudler, E. Colors, Colors? Web site: Neuroscience for Kids. URL: http:// faculty.washington.edu/chudler/words.html. Article read: May 10, 2002.

DeRosnay, J. 1998. Entropy and the Laws of Thermodynamics. Web site: Principia Cybernetica Web. URL: http://pespmc1.vub.ac.be/ ENTRTHER. HTML. Article read: May 31, 2002.

French, B. 1996. Working Memory. Web site: University of Alberta Cognitive Science Dictionary. URL: http://www.psych.ualberta. ca/~mike/Pearl_Street/Dictionary/contents/W/working_memory. html. Article read: May 10, 2002.

General Dennis J. Reimer Training and Doctrine Digital Library. Obtaining and Recording Physical Evidence. Web site: General Dennis J. Reimer Training and Doctrine Digital Library. URL: http://155.217.58.58/cgi-bin/atdl.dll/fm/19-20/ch7.htm. Article read: October 14, 2001.

Gleitman, H. et al. 1999. *Psychology*. W.W. Norton & Company, New York.

Goldman, M. Standing Waves. Web site: Physics 2000. URL: http:// www.colorado.edu/physics/2000/microwaves/standing_ wave1.html. Article read: June 10, 2002.

Henderson, T. 2001. The Doppler Effect and Shock Waves. Web site: The Physics Classroom. URL: http://www.glenbrook.k12.il.us/ gbssci/phys/Class/sound/u11l3b.html. Article read: May 25, 2002.

Miller, F. 1967. *College Physics*. Harcourt, Brace & World, Inc., New York.

Pinker, S. 1999. His Brain Measured Up. Web site: The New York Times on the Web. URL: http://www.mit.edu/~pinker/einstein.html. Article read: May 10, 2002.

Rowland, R. 2002. Firefighters and Cancer. Web site: CBC News. URL: http://cbc.ca/news/features/firefighter_safety/cancer.html. Article read: May 26, 2002.

Rowland, R. 2002. What's In Smoke? Web site: CBC News. URL: http:// cbc.ca/news/features/firefighter_safety/smoke.html. Article read: May 26, 2002.

Stockley, C. et al. 1999. *The Usborne Illustrated Dictionary of Science*. Usborne Publishing, London, England.

ScienceNet. 2002. Do identical twins have identical fingerprints? Web site: ScienceNet, Biology & Medical Science. URL: http://www.sciencenet.org.uk/database/Biology/9609/b00598d.html. Article read: May 26, 2002.

Time. 1982. *The Concord Desk Encyclopaedia*. Concord Reference Books, Inc., New York.

USGS Learning Web. 2002. Navigation. Web site: USGS Learning Web. URL: http://interactive2.usgs.gov/learningweb/teachers/exploremaps_ lesson2.htm. Article read: May 10, 2002.

USGS Learning Web. 1998. Why geologic maps are made and how they are used. Web site: USGS Learning Web. URL: http://geology.wr.usgs.gov/wgmt/whymaps.html. Article read: May 10, 2002.